Beauty and Grace

A Novel

By

James Black

Beauty and Grace is a work of fiction. Names, places, times, events and characters are all a product of the author's imagination. Any similarity to real individuals or places is coincidental.

ISBN: 9798589349788
Copyright © 2021

Dedicated to:

    Our children and their children

Edited by

Paula Ennis

Chapter 1

The Great Queen

"Do you remember what I told you about the Great Queen?" the Wizard asked J. His expression was serious as if something grave was about to happen.

J (King Calvin's oldest son) had been more interested in using the sword than listening to the Wizard about the Great Queen and Matakwa. He did remember his governess telling him bedtime stories about the Great Queen's delicious recipes.

"Yes," he replied. "I know the story. I know she created lollipop soup and banana splits."

The look on the Wizard's face grew alarmed. It was clear the boy had missed the whole point, which was, what had transpired and why the story was important.

"Do you remember the Unicorn?" the Wizard asked.

He did remember seeing the Unicorn in the Moon Pool. And he remembered how beautiful Matakwa was. But those were only images in a fantasy. "There is no such thing," replied the boy with an air of confidence. The Great Queen story was simply that. An old tale.

The Wizard grew more alarmed. "No time to waste," he said. "We must return to my cave! Now! You are not safe here in your father's palace" He grabbed the boy by the collar, rushed him into the courtyard, hoisted him up onto the Griffin's back, then mounted, and off they went.

Long ago, when the Great Queen was a young maiden, a terrible plague came upon her kingdom and all the kingdoms of the Middle World. In fact, it existed beyond the Middle World. But back then, people did not travel to other places. In fact, most never traveled more than a day away from their home. They had heard vague stories of lands beyond the sea, which surrounded the Middle World. Most had never even seen the sea. Only those living near the eastern shore, who had encountered seafarers, were aware of other lands far across the sea. Unfortunately for the peoples of the Middle World, one of those seafaring ships brought with it the plague of evil. The crew was ashore only for a short time, and encountered only one family, but that was just enough time for the plague to establish a foothold in the Middle World.

It spread from family to family, then from town to town and finally from Kingdom to Kingdom. It was very communicable.

The plague was transmitted to others via the spoken word. Yes, it is true, simply speaking would transmit the plague. Hearing evil words from the mouth of an infected person would infect a person's mind. It was within one year that most of the people in the Middle World were sick or dying.

Both of the Great Queen's parents, the King and Queen of Kambuka, died. At age 18, she became the only living heir and inherited the kingdom.

Naturally, she was grieving the loss of her parents. She loved them very much. It was a great loss for her. But beyond that grief, she now had to be ruler of the kingdom. It was the worst of all possible scenarios. No parents, young girl becomes Queen, and a terrible plague upon the land.

For three days she isolated herself in her room. Her heart was overwhelmed with sadness. Her mind was filled with hopelessness. Tears flooded down her face until she was drained. All was lost. She feared the end of the kingdom and all its citizens was at hand. She had no hope.

On the third night, overwhelmed with grief, she left the palace. Not knowing why or where she was going, she only knew she had to get away. She found herself passing through the royal gardens and following a path that led up to the top of a knoll. Not paying attention, she did not look up at the top of the knoll, which was straight ahead of her. She did not yet see the Unicorn. When she finally did look up, she was stunned at the radiance and beauty of the creature. Its mane and tail glowed silver in the light of the moon. Its horn radiated bright as the sun. She was frozen in her tracks as she stared. For the first time since her parents' death, she saw a beacon of hope. The hopelessness that had filled her heart and mind began to fade.

She moved towards the Unicorn. Her steps quickened as she moved closer. Drawn to its beauty, she felt stronger with each step. She reached out to touch the magnificent creature. Her hand rested on its neck. First her hand, then her arm, and eventually her entire body was filled with warmth. She felt great joy. With excitement and anticipation in her heart, she reached for its horn. Wrapping her hand around it, she was filled with the magical power of the Unicorn. It was as if a bolt of lightning had struck her, illuminating her mind and body. In that moment, the Great Queen realized she had the power to overcome the pandemic.

She returned to the palace with newfound confidence and determination.

"Assemble the royal advisers and captain of the guard," she called out to her royal secretary. "I will instruct them on how to overcome the plague."

When all were assembled, she gave them instructions on what to do, then sent them out to all four corners of Kambuka. Citizens were cautioned to stay in their homes. Most importantly, they were not to speak to others outside their immediate family. This was the only way to prevent the pandemic from spreading. It took several weeks for the Great Queen's orders to be fully implemented. Once done, however, the pandemic began to subside. Those infected had to remain in quarantine for two weeks. One year passed before the pandemic was eradicated from the kingdom.

Once the healing of Kambuka had begun, the Great Queen traveled to neighboring kingdoms in the western half of the Middle World. As she had done in Kambuka, she called for the advisers and captains to assemble. They too were given instructions and sent out to eradicate the plague. Many of the Kings and Queens had already succumbed to the plague, leaving the Great Queen to rule their kingdoms too. It took more than a decade for life to return to normal. By that time, the Great Queen ruled much of the western Middle World.

Her reign was a time of peace and prosperity. Young couples married and started families. Towns grew into cities. Crops flourished, creating an abundance of food. The Great Queen even created new recipes. She was known throughout the land for her lollipop soup and banana splits. Children of Kambuka learned to fly and animals learned to speak. For fifty years she reigned. For fifty years there were no wars. No pandemics. Just happiness and prosperity.

The Great Queen married very late in life. Her husband was a commoner with whom she fell deeply in love. He was very handsome and smart but had no royal title. This did not matter to her but did cause some grumbling among the nobles who wanted *their* son to marry her. As it turned out, the Great Queen had only one child. A beautiful girl. All the Middle World celebrated her birth. Sadly, that joy turned to sorrow when the Great Queen fell ill. The girl child was only a month old when her mother died. Some thought it was a complication from her pregnancy, which happened so late in life. There were rumors of poison. The truth was that evil had never really left the Middle World. It had gone into hiding. Waiting for the right time to return. In her old age and weakened from childbirth, evil, in the form of the plague, sneaked into her royal apartments and infected her. But this time, it did not spread as widely as before. The Great Queen stayed in isolation, which prevented the plague from spreading. Knowing her end was near, she wrote a note to her most trusted adviser that he was to summon his fellow advisers from each kingdom. They were instructed to find suitable heirs of former Kings and Queens to become future rulers. She met with each of the future possible rulers. She did not speak directly to them for fear of spreading the disease. Instead, her instructions on how to prevent the plague from ravaging their kingdoms were written out and handed to the possible rulers by herself. This way they knew it was the Great Queen and not someone else "speaking" to them. It would prove to be very difficult, for the new rulers did not have the Great Queen's power. People would not always trust and obey their new King or Queen.

The future rulers knew this and knew it was the Great Queen's power that held all the kingdoms together. There were rumors about the Unicorn. A few wanted its power for themselves. Giving them the power was not to be. The Great Queen suspected they would misuse the power, causing strife and discord. Moreover, it would empower selfish rulers. Selfish rulers were just what the plague wanted. It would use them to spread evil, instead of stopping it.

The Great Queen suspected this would happen. She did not tell them they could not have the power. She told them to wait until she passed beyond this life, and then the power would be passed on properly. "Properly" meant she would return the power to the Unicorn's horn. There it would reside until her heir was ready. She told the Unicorn:

Unto you, dear Unicorn, I bequeath my power, to hold and protect within your horn. Hold it until my heir is ready. You will know her by her beautiful spirit and golden hair. She is destined to receive my power, and rule as I have, with Beauty and Grace.

The Unicorn had left Kambuka, returning to the safety of the Silver Mountains, before the Great Queen's death. After her funeral, a few of the new rulers searched for the Unicorn, to acquire its power. Alas, they were unsuccessful. Over the centuries, the power of the Great Queen and the Unicorn became lost in legend and tales. Only Wizards knew that the story was true.

As they flew, J asked the Wizard, "What does the Great Queen have to do with us?"

"Nothing," said the Wizard. "It is evil you need to be worried about."

"Evil?" asked J. "What does evil have to do with anything?" The Wizard, still frustrated that J had not listened very well before, answered,

J, as I have previously told you, the pandemic came from a land beyond the sea, causing suffering and death. It was the Great Queen's power that stopped it and brought peace and prosperity. Well, there are signs that evil is gathering strength and will bring the plague again. We must be prepared to stop it.

Chapter 2

The Moon Pool

It was a short flight from the palace in Kambuka to the Wizard's cave. With great haste, the Wizard jumped off the Griffin, ran into the cave, and called for the girl.

"Raven, Raven, where is Raven?" he called out.

"Who is Raven?" asked J.

"The Girl, young one. The Girl, along with you, who will save the Middle World from the plague to come."

J was confused. How could he possibly save anything? And who was Raven? What did she have to do with anything? Was that the same girl he had met in the cave before?

J followed the Wizard into the cave. There seemed to be a flurry of activity. People were coming and going. Noise was everywhere. As the Wizard passed, however, people stopped talking. They stood still and watched him. He seemed to possess a great power to command respect. J tried to make sense of all this but did not have much luck.

They passed the giant room with the beautiful lights and the reflecting pool. J remembered what the girl told him the last time they passed the reflecting pool:

> You will see things about yourself. About the man you are to become. About your future. The Wizard will know when it is time for you to peer into the reflecting pool.

They went on into the small room containing the Moon Pool. In that pool, J had seen the Unicorn. He had seen Matakwa and her beauty. He remembered the moonlight radiating in her golden hair. He saw them fly away.

"Look," said the Wizard. "Look into the Moon Pool."

This time J saw children playing. He saw them laughing and running here and there.

"Look deeper," urged the Wizard. This time, J saw a dark cloud forming.

"What is that?" J asked.

"Evil," replied the Wizard.

The Wizard spoke no more words. He left J at the Moon Pool, in which J also saw his own reflection. He was alone, to ponder the day's events.

The Wizard gathered the other wizards, warriors, wise men, and wise women in the cave together. They sat in high back chairs arranged in a circle around the reflecting pool. Each was wearing a necklace of their Order. Wizards had magical stones in their necklaces. Warriors had small replicas of their weapons, like swords, lances, and maces. The wise men and women wore only simple necklaces.

There were quiet conversations in hushed tones. They were somber. No one smiled.

"You all know why we are here," the Wizard said in a solemn tone. "We must make haste with stealth if we are going to prevent evil from spreading another pandemic. We must get the Boy and Girl to the Unicorn before evil grows beyond our capacity to stop it. They are our only hope."

Everyone in the room nodded in agreement. One of the other wizards, who wore a brilliant diamond on his necklace, spoke. "How are we to get them to the Unicorn? Evil will see us coming and send the plague to us."

"That is why we have to travel in secrecy," replied the Wizard. "Our party must be small. Only a few travelers. Unremarkable. Traveling to the Silver Mountains for the celebration of ...." Before he could finish his statement, one of the warriors rose and blurted out,

"How many should be in the party?"

"One each, a wizard, a warrior, a wise man and a wise woman in addition to the Boy and Girl," answered the Wizard.

"Are you sure the boy and girl are the Chosen Ones? This could be very dangerous if they are not," said one of the wise men.

In those days, a "boy" was a "boy" until he had experienced his Nach-Ny-Don-Qua. In J's case, he was actually about to have his 20th birthday. "Girls" remained "girls" until they married or had an experience similar to Nach-Ny-Don-Qua. Since neither J nor the Girl (who was a year older than J) had had such an experience, they were still "boy" and "girl".

"The reflecting pool speaks the truth. We shall have the Boy and Girl look into the pool. There, they will foresee their role in this vital matter," said the Wizard.

All in the room agreed with the Wizard. J and the girl were brought to the pool. The assembly sat in their high back chairs watching. J was ushered to the pool first.

"Look deep. Look into your future. The pool will tell you if you are one of the Chosen," spoke the Wizard gravely.

J stepped to the edge of the pool. He hesitated and looked at the Wizard, who nodded for him to look. He was afraid. The girl stepped up next to J. She took his hand in hers.

"I am here, with you. We will venture forward together. You and I. Companions in whatever may come." Her words were reassuring. He looked into her eyes. J saw her commitment to both him and the task ahead. With a slight smile, he turned and gazed into the pool.

At first, he saw only his and her reflections. Slowly, other images began to form. He saw great snowcapped mountains. He saw a tranquil valley, filled with trees bearing fruits of all types and lush grass. Standing on a knoll was the Unicorn, tall and proud. Its tail and mane were glowing in the sunlight. Suddenly, the sky darkened, menacing clouds formed, lightning cracked, and pounding rain poured down. Thunder crashed with such force; J tore his eyes away from the pool in mortal fear.

"It's all right," the girl said. Her voice was calm and reassuring. "I am here." J looked at her. She saw extreme fear in his eyes. "We will face this together."

"I am not sure I can go there," J said.

"You can and you must!" insisted the girl.

She continued, "Remember what Winston taught you when he brought you to the Wizard's cave. You did not want to ride him. As I recall, you wanted to fly and not ride on a mule. But he taught you many things on that trip, not the least of which was about fear. He told you 'Fear is your friend. No one likes to feel afraid. Fear, however, can be a good friend. It can keep you safe'."

J looked at her. "How did you know that? How can you know what Winston told me on the way here? No one was there but Winston and me."

"I am much more than a little girl," she replied. "I have gazed into the Moon Pool more than once. I know what must be done and who must do it."

"What?" J asked. "What must be done? What is my purpose in all this?"

The Girl smiled but did not reply. The Wizard put his hand on J's shoulder and said, "You have seen enough for one day. Rest." He ushered J into a corner of the room where he could see the proceedings but not be directly involved.

"It is settled," said the Wizard. "The party shall be the Boy and Girl, a wizard, warrior, wise man and woman. Who among us shall be in the party?"

There was general consensus that the Wizard should go. Several of the warriors volunteered. Each wanted to share in the glory of subduing evil. This troubled the wise men and especially the wise women. This undertaking was not about glory. It was about saving the Middle World. If a warrior were seeking only glory, he might jeopardize the entire mission. There was one warrior who did not sit with the others in the circle around the Moon Pool. He stood quietly in the shadows. He was known as Ranger. Rae, a wise woman, looked at him and spoke.

"Ranger should accompany the group," she announced.

Except for the volunteer warriors, all the other participants in the circle looked at Ranger, then nodded their heads in agreement. Two of the volunteer warriors rose and stomped out in anger. It was very good they would not be in the party.

"I propose Rae represent the wise women," said the wise woman sitting next to her. Rae was in her 30's. Her body was lean and athletic. Her fingers were long and thin, as were her other features. Clearly, she could travel great distances on foot, if necessary. She was also known to be protective of those she cared for. Again, all the participants nodded in agreement.

There were several moments of silence following Rae's joining the party. None of the wise men volunteered. No one else suggested a wise man to join them. It seemed as if the party would be short one person. It was the Girl who broke the silence.

"I have gazed into the Moon Pool more than once. I saw our party leave with five, not six. But when we arrived at the Silver Mountains, there were six."

"So it shall be," said the Wizard. "The Fellowship of Five will arrive as the Circle of Six. The Circle, never ending, all connected by a common purpose."

There were nods and words of agreement among those gathered. It was settled. They would leave in two days. That would give them time to prepare for the trip.

The next day, preparations began. Food, clothing, and weapons were carefully packed. J wanted to bring a sword for himself. However, the Wizard forbade it.

"Have you forgotten everything I told you? First you must master Beauty and Grace. After that, you will need to learn how NOT to use a weapon. Only then will you be ready for a sword," admonished the Wizard. J wanted to argue with him, but he knew better.

That evening a banquet was planned. Unbeknownst to J, Naomi had been brought to the cave. She had prepared J's favorites, including lollipop soup. After being seated next to the girl at the head of the table, J saw Naomi carrying in a tureen full of his favorite soup.

"Couldna let young mas-ser go-a trapsin' off ta some wild mountin hungry," she said. "Sides, not fittn' to send ur Circle off wit out ta proper sendin' hoff. Now eat up, cause ur gonna needn' to be ready for the morrow."

Then she hollered out to all at the grand banquet table, "Y'all return dis here young master fit as a fiddle ta me or ur gonna feel the wrath of Naomi!!!!," she warned.

J smiled as he took a large helping of lollipop soup. He was surely going to miss Naomi's food. On the other hand, he would not miss her constant reminders of what he should and should not do.

The banquet was a somber affair. Guests were there to support the Circle and wish them well. Several spoke touching words of farewell to J, the Girl, the Wizard, Ranger, and Rae.

James Black

Chapter 3

The Journey Begins

Early the next morning, J was awakened by Naomi shaking him.

"Get urself up, lil J. Your jour-nee begins. Today ur gonna beg-in ur path to man-a-hood." She fed him a full breakfast of eggs, bacon, toast, waffles, fresh fruit, orange juice, and milk. By the time he finished, his stuffed stomach ached.

"Teach ya ta be makin' ah pig ah da self," she scolded him. J smiled and said, "I love you too, Naomi." Tears flooded down her cheeks. Her face was flushed. "Luv ta too," she replied, hugging him and kissing his cheek. Then she ran off before her wails could be heard. Her heart ached with sadness. J would never again be the boy she had raised with so much love. She knew the day would come when he would set out to find his way in the world. Even so, knowing did not lessen her heartache.

The Circle made their way to the cave's entrance among well-wishers who lined the way out. Winston was waiting, loaded with baggage. There were five ponies, saddled and ready to go. J felt much better seeing Winston. He went to the mule, petted him and said, "Good to see you, my friend." Winston snorted. It was clear J had forgotten the lesson Winston had taught him that humans could be friends with other humans, but not with animals.

The Circle rode east, riding up the road that zigzagged back and forth up the mountain pass. When they reached the summit, the Wizard halted to rest the ponies. J went up to Winston and stroked his neck.

"I am very glad you are with us," J told Winston, feeling the need to tell the mule again. Winston snorted, then said, "Naomi told me to keep you safe. She said I would make a fine pot roast if I didn't."

A huge grin spread across J's face. "Well, you better do what Naomi says. She is not someone to trifle with." Winston nodded as mules do with their heads raising and lowering several times, then snorting.

The Circle started out with the Wizard in the lead. He was followed by Rae and Ranger. J rode alongside the Girl with Winston bringing up the rear. There was a long silence. J said, "You never told me your name." "True, I didn't," the Girl replied. Another silence while J waited for her to tell him her name. Which she did not. Finally, he asked her, "Why did the Wizard call you Raven? Is that your name?" To which she replied, "That is one of my names." This confused J. In Kambuka, people had only one name.

Calvin, Naomi, J, G, A, even Ponakwa had only one name. J decided that further conversation would not be beneficial, so he slowed down, waiting for Winston.

"Winston?" J asked, "why does the Girl keep to herself?" Winston, being Winston, answered J's question with a question, "Why do YOU think she is that way?"

J thought for a few minutes, then said, "When we first arrived at the Wizard's cave, I thought she was a servant. She did not act as if she were anyone of importance. But when we got to the Moon Pool and she told me not to look into it, I began to think she was not a servant. She spoke as a person who knew things a servant would never know, such as the power of the Moon Pool. Now, being a member of the Circle, she must be much more than an ordinary Girl."

Winston listened to J with interest. "You are right, J, she is more than an ordinary Girl. If you want to know about her, wait. You have asked with no success. When she is ready to tell you, she will. Your task is to be patient." This was not what J wanted to hear. His natural tendency was to rush in, demand answers, and not stop until he got what he sought. A natural tendency for boys his age.

J was beginning to learn about patience. He took Winston's advice and waited. The party continued down the east side of the mountain for most of the day. It was almost dark when they came to a grassy clearing next to a small stream. The water was ice cold and sparkling clear. Each member, the ponies, and Winston took long drinks.

"We will camp here tonight," decided the Wizard. "Can't we go to an Inn?" asked J. "No, we cannot. We cannot be seen. Our trip must be a secret. If evil gets wind of us, it will use dastardly means to stop us." J was not happy. He wanted to fill his tummy with a delicious dinner, then snuggle into a warm comfy bed. That was not to be. Instead, he ate a cold dinner and slept on the hard ground. It was good that Winston had taught him how to find a good sleeping place outside, when they took their trip to the Wizard's cave. J was beginning to see the benefit of riding to the cave instead of flying. He was learning many valuable lessons.

Before dawn, Rae shook J out of his slumber. "Rise and shine," she said with a chipper voice. J peeked out from under his blankets to see her smiling face. "What is for breakfast?" he asked. "I don't know. However, Naomi packed it so I am sure it will be nourishing," she replied. J was not convinced. He imagined a stack of warm pancakes swimming in maple syrup, and hot chocolate, not cold oatmeal and an apple. Well, at least the stream would prove to be refreshing.

"I understand you wanted to know about the Girl," said Rae. "She is complicated. Her life was not like yours."

"You know about my life?" asked J. "Yes. We have been following your life from before you were born," she replied.

"Before I was born?" J said, confused. "Yes. The Moon Pool revealed your birth and childhood."

"Did it show my future too?"

"No. That is for you to discover."

Rae began to tell J about the Girl. She was born of royalty but raised under other circumstances. As she started telling the details, the Wizard interrupted.

"Time for talk later. We don't have time to waste," he said.

During the night, the Wizard had disturbing dreams. They predicted that evil had already spread much faster than expected. When he woke up, a gray hawk was sitting on a tree limb above him.

"What have you seen?" asked the Wizard. The hawk had traveled far to the east. It had flown over the great forest, over untended wheat fields, to the village beyond. There, it found great strife among the people. Illness was starting to spread already. The Wizard had dreamt about this, but was dismayed to learn that evil had traveled so far from the eastern shore. It was over 100 leagues away. There was no time to waste. The Circle must get to the kingdom before evil gained control.

They ate without conversation, saddled their ponies and headed east, following the stream. It was a lovely day. The sun was warm, sky was deep blue. The Circle could not help but enjoy the beauty of the day. Rae and the Girl had formed a special bond. They rode together, speaking softly. Both had been raised under similar circumstances. However, they had very different parents. The Girl's parents were royalty. They were King and Queen of the Northern Kingdom. Rae's parents were in the same kingdom, but not royalty. They were intelligentsia.

It was foretold a Girl child would be born of royal parents. Her birth would occur during a blue moon. When the blue moon was highest in the sky, the Unicorn would fly across, casting its moon shadow over the newborn Girl child. As it happened, the Girl's parents were returning to the palace when birth pains began. The carriage was well built, but the road was rough. The bumps jostled and jerked the King and Queen. Suddenly, the Queen cried out, "Stop the carriage! I can't take the pain." A bed was hastily arranged for her. The sun had set hours before and the moon was rising to its fullness. The Queen's contractions were becoming stronger and much more painful. She cried out time and again in pain. Finally, with all her might, the Queen gave one final push and the Girl emerged into the world. No sooner had she been born than the moonlight darkened. The King and Queen looked up to see the Unicorn flying in front of the moon, darkening the sky. He was magnificent. His wings floated through the sky with grace and beauty. His horn shimmered in the moonlight, as did his mane and tail. The prophecy was fulfilled. But there was more to the prophecy, and it was not good.

The King knew of the prophecy and became very worried for his daughter's safety. "Tell no one of this," he ordered the entourage. None did. It was kept a secret.

The King knew that his daughter was destined to thwart evil. Both King and Queen were proud, but worried too. It was also foretold that evil would try to kill her. So, when she was a few months old, her parents sent her to live with an older couple who lived deep in the woods. A place far from harm. The couple was very wise. They chose to live a quiet life, away from people, where they could appreciate nature and learn from the animals of the forest. This was the ideal situation for the Girl. She would be raised away from danger and in a very loving home. The couple did not have any other children, so they could lavish all their love on her.

When she was three years old, she began to play with some of the animals in the forest. A rabbit family became her favorite. She would visit their home in a small burrow hollowed under an old oak tree. The old couple gave her carrots and peas to take to her rabbit friends. There were several young rabbits, which were like brothers and sisters to her. They would all play together in the meadow just beyond their tree home. They snuggled together in the shade of the old oak tree and took long afternoon naps. Even in the winter, she would visit with them. But the weather was too cold for naps. So, the rabbits would come to her cottage and they would snuggle together in blankets by the fireplace. The woman would give the Girl hot chocolate and the rabbits carrots.

She learned the ways of forest animals. The rabbits taught her how to watch and listen for danger. She learned the meaning of each sound and different smells of the forest. Some smells were wonderful. Flowers blooming, and the scent of pine trees made her happy to be part of the forest's beauty. The rabbit family also taught her to listen to the birds. Birds were always on the lookout for danger. She could tell by their songs when danger was near. She also learned to sing their songs. They had songs telling where food could be found, when it was time to fly south for the winter, and when to mate. She especially liked the sounds of cardinals. Small, with very red feathers, they would sing back to her when she imitated their songs.

Cardinals don't migrate, so they know the forest very well. The Girl would always know what was going on in the forest by listening to them. She knew each of their songs. There were songs warning of a predator, songs giving an all clear after it left, songs directing where to find food, announcing their return to their nests with food, even calling for their mate to come back to the nest. The songs were all similar. The Girl had to listen very carefully to tell which song it was. Eventually, she learned that a high chirp at the beginning of the song meant one thing while that same high chirp at the end meant something quite different.

As the troupe rode into the forest, the Girl listened for bird songs. She was especially keen to hear the cardinals sing. She became worried when she heard only songs of danger. It was not predator danger. Not bigger birds or larger animals that the songs were about. It was more sinister. Like a forest fire or great flood. It was evil! The Girl rode ahead to warn the Wizard. He too was aware of the bird songs.

"They sing of approaching danger, not danger that is here yet," he told the Girl. "We are safe from evil for the moment." Even so, the Wizard picked up the pace, coaxing his pony into a trot. The others followed him closely, and soon they were deep in the forest. Winston, being Winston, complained about the pace. Being a mule, he was not susceptible to the pandemic. It only affected humans. The Wizard was following a game trail, not the road. It took twists and turns, unlike a road. That was good because it kept the Circle hidden. At noon, they stopped for lunch and water. J was getting sore from riding and glad to stop. He was also hungry. More cold food. "When will I ever get a decent meal?" he wondered. The Wizard did not let the Circle linger. "Time to start riding," he said. He pushed the troupe harder. By evening they had traveled many leagues and were nearing the edge of the forest. They stopped to pitch camp before nightfall.

The birds became silent. "Hush, be quiet," the Girl warned the company. "Listen," she said. Ranger whispered, "I don't hear anything." "That is the point," replied the Girl. "The birds and other creatures are all silent. That means humans are near." They all stood very still, listening intently.

"Whaaa dat?" a voice said. "Don-a know," replied a different voice. "Smells like meat," said the first voice. "Don-a smell nuttin'," said the second. No one in the Circle moved. They barely even took a breath. The smell of unwashed men wafted their way. Ranger knew they were lucky to be downwind of the men. "Tis over dis-a way," said the first voice. "Fall-er me." The voice faded in the distance.

"We are too close to the road," said the Wizard. "We must move farther into the forest." After a short time, the birds began to sing the all clear song. "It is ok now," said the Girl. "Who were those men?" asked Rae. "Trappers from the north," said Ranger. "Probably were lost. We are quite a ways from the road," he added. J remembered what Winston had said about getting lost. He remembered that animals don't get lost. Only humans get lost. The birds began singing their nighttime songs. Songs that called their mates to come back to the nests for the night. "We can sleep here tonight," said the Girl. "The birds will sound an alarm if the men come back." They did stay the night there. But none of the Circle slept well. They were too busy listening.

As it turned out, the two men were lost. They were hunting deer, following the same game trail the Circle was following. The men had taken a wrong turn, fortunately for the Circle, and were trying to find their way back. In doing so, they circled around nearby where the troupe was. When they found the game trail again, they were far west of the troupe.

"Do you think evil was with them?" J asked the Wizard. "Perhaps, but I doubt it. They seemed to be naturally foul men, not infected with the pandemic. We need to avoid people. One reason is we might become infected. The second is if our location is known, it might be passed on to the evil. That can happen even if people don't intend to tell. Just being in a tavern, talking about seeing our Circle, could alert bad company. Now try to get some sleep," the Wizard told J.

He did try and was more successful than the others.

Chapter 4

Ranger and the Wizard

The next morning, once again he was awakened before dawn. This time, by Ranger. "Did you get any sleep last night?" J asked him. "No, I set up a position in that tree, pointing to a large fir tree, and watched over our camp." Apparently, rangers can go several days without sleep. J began to see why Ranger was chosen to be a member of the Circle. He was quiet and unassuming, as well as a good guard. He wanted to know more. "How did you come to be a ranger?" asked J. "We can talk as we ride," Ranger replied. "Eat first." J had another breakfast of cold oatmeal. He was really getting tired of oatmeal.

It began to rain. At first, it was a light drizzle. Then the rain became heavier. Being thickly clustered in the forest, the tree leaves caught much of the rain. But when the wind blew, water showered off the leaves, soaking everyone in the Circle. Fortunately, Naomi had packed a rain slicker for J. It was dark brown, the color of the trees, which made J almost invisible. It also kept him warm and dry. Only his hands, which held the pony's reins, were cold and wet. From time to time, he would slip one of his hands inside the slicker's pocket to warm it up.

J rode beside Ranger for most of the morning. Ranger did not seem to be bothered by the cold and rain. He told J about growing up in the south. He did *not* tell J that his true heritage was in the Eastern Kingdom. He knew Sanders. They were from the same city. "I am glad that Sanders and Ponakwa are married. They will make a fine couple," he said. He liked living in the south, where it was warm all winter. "Especially on days like today," he added. "We would get rain, sometimes very heavy, but it was not cold like today."

Ranger's story went way back. It began centuries before he was born. His ancestors had ruled the Eastern Kingdom. During the time of the Great Queen, evil plagued the Kingdom. J had heard very little about the "time of the Great Queen". He wanted to ask about it but decided to wait. Better to not interrupt a good story. Most of the royal family had succumbed to the pandemic, as did much of the population. Only the King's daughter survived. She was taken to the Valley of the Unicorn for safety. The King's advisers established an interim government to run the Kingdom until the royal heir came to claim the throne. Over the years, many pretenders tried to claim the throne. These pretenders claimed royal heritage, and even had documents (forged) showing their lineage. The true heir, it was prophesied, would come to claim the throne only after evil was driven from the Kingdom forever!

"Are you the true heir?" asked J.

"We shall see," said Ranger. Although, he really knew he was. It was destiny that brought him to the Wizard's cave. It was destiny that Ranger joined the Circle. And it was destiny that he was to travel to the Valley of the Unicorn.

A strong gust of wind came up, blowing buckets of rain off the tree leaves. The game trail became a muddy bog. The ponies' hooves sank into the mud up to their knees. The Wizard wanted to halt until the game trail dried, but the Girl said, "Follow me. I will lead you." J saw a raven flying just ahead of her. It seemed to be speaking to her. He was reminded that the Wizard had called out, "Raven, Raven, where is Raven." Was he calling for this raven or was he calling for the Girl?

"Follow me," the raven chirped to the Girl. "I know the way."

She led the way. The rest of the Fellowship of Five followed. They wound through the forest, avoiding muddy bogs, finding solid, firm ground to ride on.

"Tell me about the Wizard," J asked Ranger, feeling closer to him now that he knew where Ranger grew up. "I don't even know his name."

"The Wizard has many names," Ranger replied. "I first met him growing up in the Southern Kingdom. Ranger continued,

> There, he is known as Bayaz, which means bright, white, and dazzling. The King of the Southern Kingdom invited him to the Silver Jubilee celebration of the King's reign. When I first saw him, he looked as he does today, tall, thin, long gray beard. As children, we wondered if he had been born with a beard. People said they had never seen him without it. When he was with us children, his eyes were warm and comforting. We would follow him around wherever he went.

> We did not understand why adults feared him. He was always kind to me and the other children. One time he put his hand on my shoulder and whispered in my ear, "One day, you will claim your throne."

Ranger went on to tell J that adults feared Bayaz. He continued,

> Maybe it was because of his magical power. Maybe it was because he was a stranger. His eyes were not warm and comforting when he looked at adults. Later, I found out all wizards are that way. One has to be careful when in the presence of a wizard.

After the Silver Jubilee banquet, at nightfall, Bayaz set off his dazzling fireworks display. It began with an explosion of lightning bolts thundering from the sky. They struck the ground with a deafening roar, emitting a brilliant white light. People dropped to the ground and covered their heads for fear of their lives. Bayaz revelled at the sight.

It took several minutes for calm to return. When it did, people thought the display was over. It was not. Out of the north another bolt of lightning and crash and thunder roared. Looking up, everyone first saw a dazzling bright white light. As it faded, they saw a unicorn, flying high in the sky. It left a glittering rainbow as it passed over.

This time, people marveled and applauded at the beautiful sight. Bayaz's fireworks display would be remembered in song and story.

"You said he is known by many names. What are his other names?" J asked Ranger. "In the north, he is known as Flokerviss, a wise guardian of the people."

"How did he come by *that* name?" J asked. Ranger continued,

Dragons live in the North. One in particular, Asmun, had been terrorizing many villages and towns. He would swoop down, belching fire, burning houses, crops, even livestock. He would have done the same to the people if they had not hidden in underground bunkers. A messenger was sent to Flokerviss begging for help. Heeding their pleas, he came to their aid. His motives were not just to save the people. Asmun had, as all dragons did, a treasure of gold and rare jewels. One jewel in particular, known as the Diamond of Asmun, was coveted by Flokerviss. This diamond had magical powers. It is the very diamond you have seen on his staff.

Flokerviss knew the only way he could defeat the dragon was to use guile. So, he went to Asmun's cave. Standing at the cave's mouth, he called out, "Asmun, I have a riddle for you." That piqued the dragon's interest. "Speak now or die!" demanded the dragon. "It is not just any riddle. It is a riddle in a limerick. If you get the correct answer you can burn me alive. But if you don't, you must grant me two wishes," Flokerviss said. Here is the limerick riddle:

Turn it around and you will see.

And, when you do, best to flee.

NU-M-SA it is called.

Get too near and it will scald!

Do you know the name, can you tell me?

"That is easy," said Asmun, "it is *Dragon*.

"Wrong!" declared Flokerviss. "Try again."

Asmun thought for a few minutes. He concentrated on his next answer. "I have it," he declared with confidence. "It is *fire!*"

"Wrong again! What is your last guess?"

This time Asmun thought long and hard. Steam emerged from around the edges of his mouth as his anger and frustration grew. After several minutes, a sly smile drew across his face. "I have it," he said. "It is ME!" he declared with supreme confidence.

"Are you sure that is your answer?" asked Flokerviss with a slight quiver of apprehension in his voice. Supremely confident, Asmun answered, "Absolutely!".

"Wrong! The answer is your name ASMUN. Spelled backwards is it NU-M-SA."

Asmun was outraged, declaring "Me" was his name. Flokerviss was not deterred.

"You lost! Now you must grant me my two wishes. First, never again terrorize these people. Second, I want the Asmun Diamond."

Asmun could, reluctantly, abide by the first wish, but the second one cut him to the core. He loved that diamond. Parting with it was more than he could bear. Trying to use guile on the Wizard, he tried to substitute a different diamond. Flokerviss recognized the deception immediately. After hemming and hawing, Asmun finally gave up his diamond. From that day on, the Wizard was known as Flokerviss because his wisdom protected the people from Asmun.

"Does the Wizard have other names?" J asked, hoping there were none. He was tired of listening to long stories.

"He does," replied Ranger. "Here he is known as Alvar, which means warrior/leader of a magical army."

The raven they had been following led them to the edge of the forest. When they finally emerged from the trees, they could see the sun was shining. The clouds were gone. The Circle stopped and dismounted. It was time for food and rest.

Chapter 5

Matakwa

As the Circle rested and ate their lunch, a raven flew down and landed next to the Girl. She shared her bread with the bird. It squawked several notes to her. She nodded in understanding.

"What did the raven say?" asked Rae.

"Trouble ahead. Evil has infected two villages. The inhabitants are plagued with the disease. It is not safe to get near them."

"How badly are they infected?" Rae queried.

"Not extremely bad. There is still time for hope. The plague has not established a firm foothold," replied the Girl.

At this point, Alvar the Wizard decided it was the right time to tell J about the nature of the pandemic and his role in its eradication.

"J," he said, "the pandemic affects people's minds. It works its way into their thinking and causes them to entertain and obsess on negative thoughts. Rather than see the good in something, they see only the bad. For example, we just passed through a cold wet forest. We could consider that as bad. However, would we have had the raven guide us and warn us about the villages ahead if we had not been there?" Alvar continued,

Once a person's mind is infected, their body follows. They imagine all the illnesses they can get, and soon they can even manifest symptoms. Some will die just as a result of believing they are deathly ill. Your destiny is to rid the Middle World of the pandemic, once and for all."

"How can I do that? I am only a boy." J asked. Alvar spoke words J would remember all his life,

True, you are only a boy. But not just any boy. You are the CHOSEN BOY, just as Raven is the CHOSEN GIRL. Together, you will overcome the pandemic and restore peace to the Middle World. You will have the power within both of you. Together, you will heal villages. But you are way too weak right now to fight the pandemic. In fact, it would overcome both of you. That is why we are going to the Valley of the Unicorn. Recall the story of the Great Queen. On her deathbed, she placed her power in the Unicorn's horn. We are traveling to the valley where you will take that horn in your hands and reclaim the power. Together, you and Raven will then be stronger than the pandemic. Together, you will drive evil out of the Middle

World. But first we must get you to the Valley of the Unicorn.

J was stunned. He had no idea of his destiny. No idea he was the Chosen One. He had thought the Girl was a servant. Now, he learns she is Raven, the other Chosen One. He thought the Unicorn was only a mythical character in a fairy tale.

"And what about Matakwa?" he thought. "Her name keeps coming up. What does she have to do with all this?"

"You probably want to know about Matakwa too," said Alvar.

"Matakwa, as you may recall, was the great-great-great-granddaughter of the Great Queen."

J remembered his vision of Matakwa in the Moon Pool. He had seen her ride the Unicorn and fly away. There was something he vaguely remembered about Beauty and Grace. But he did not recall what it had to do with the vision in the Moon Pool. At the time, he had been more interested in swords.

The Wizard continued, "The Great Queen passed on her power. You may recollect what she said on her deathbed."

"Unto you, dear Unicorn, I bequeath my power, to hold and protect within your horn. Hold it until my heiress is ready. You will know her by her beautiful spirit and golden hair. She is destined to receive my power, and rule as I have, with Beauty and Grace."

Matakwa was the heiress. She, like Raven, was born of royalty but raised by a loving couple deep in the woods. At the age of maturity, she returned to the palace and took her rightful place as Princess of the realm. The same realm in which your father, Calvin, is King. During her time as Princess and later as Queen, she brought Beauty and Grace to the kingdom. Her beauty was within her. She saw only the good in all living things. She was admired throughout the kingdom for her ability to resolve differences. Especially over matters of State. Disputes were common among leaders. One often-told story concerned two villages.

The villages shared a common pasture. The dispute was over grazing rights. Each village accused the other of overgrazing. The village of Anasasieo (An-ah-sa-see-o) accused the village of Bynokie (By-no-kee) of letting their cows eat too much grass. Bynokie accused Anasasieo's sheep of doing the same thing.

When Matakwa arrived, the leaders (called Burgermeisters) were in the process of calling their villagers to arms. This was not good. Matakwa told the Burgermeister of Anasasieo to bring one of Bynokie's cows to the village square. The Burgermeister was proud to bring a Bynokie cow into his village. He thought it made him look powerful. Matakwa then went to Bynokie's Burgermeister and told him to bring one of Anasasieo's sheep to their town square. Because she was the Princess, and guarded by royal soldiers, the Burgermeister had to follow her orders.

On the second day, she again ordered each Burgermeister to bring one of the other village's animals into the town square. On the third day, villagers began to complain. They had to feed and water the other village's animals in their OWN town square. Matakwa listened to their complaints. Then, she ordered them to bring yet another animal into the town square. This continued for seven days. By then, villagers were very upset. Bringing food and water to the other village's animals was becoming exhausting and very irritating.

On the eighth day, Matakwa told the Burgermeisters to return all the animals to the common pasture. After this, there was peace in the villages and no more complaints over grazing rights.

The Wizard continued telling J about Matakwa.

Often Matakwa would wake up in the night. Especially on a night with a full moon. Unable to sleep, she would make her way out of the royal apartments, down the stairs of the palace, out the garden doors, and up to the very same knoll the Great Queen had ascended.

On those full moon nights, the Unicorn would be waiting for her, his mane and tail shimmering in the moonlight. Matakwa would leap up onto his back. No bridle or saddle. She clenched onto the tuft of hair at the base of his mane. With a mighty leap, the Unicorn would bound up into the sky and off they would go.

They would survey the kingdom from high up in the air. Then, when they came to a troubled village or city, he would swoop low, showing Matakwa exactly where the strife was. She loved their night flights, as did much of the kingdom. People would come out of their houses to see the Beauty and Grace of Matakwa and the Unicorn. Her golden hair, like his mane and tail, shimmered in the moonlight.

Then Alvar taught J a lesson.

Matakwa's beauty was within her. It was an ability to see the good in life, in people, events, and things. Grace is acting on that Beauty. Seeing Beauty is necessary for one to lead the most fulfilling life. Grace is defined as the actions of a beautiful person to make the Middle World a better place.

"You," he said to J,

have Beauty within you. Grace, you must practice. Your destiny is to bring grace to the Middle World. You and Raven will drive the evil pandemic from our shores. That is your destiny. That is your Grace.

The Circle emerged from the forest, finding themselves at the top of a small hill overlooking the two villages the raven had told them about. They stopped to rest and decide what to do next. The Circle was conflicted. On the one hand, some wanted to send J and Raven into the villages. Because the pandemic had not secured a strong foothold, J and Raven could drive it out, healing the villages. On the other hand, the concern was that evil would become aware of their presence and try to force their retreat back to Alvar's cave.

"What do you think?" the Wizard asked Raven. She replied,

J and I should go in. Rae can pretend to be our guardian, who is escorting us back to our home. That way, our presence will not arouse suspicion. Just a woman and two children. We should begin by healing the children. Then, it can spread from them to the parents and other adults. It will appear to happen naturally. Then it can spread to the other village.

Alvar asked Ranger and Rae if they agreed with Raven. Both nodded in agreement. It was late afternoon which made seeking an Inn for the night perfect sense. J, of course, was more than happy to spend the night inside, with a good meal and warm bed.

"How will we heal the children?" asked J. With a smile, Raven replied, "Beauty and Grace."

Chapter 6

The Village

The trio, Rae, Raven, and J, rode their ponies into the village. They found the stables and boarded them for the night. The stable owner was not there, only a young boy. "We have three ponies that need hay and grooming," said Rae. The boy appeared to be frightened of strangers. He nodded and led the ponies inside. J followed him in. "Our ponies have had a hard day. Would it be possible to give each an apple?" J asked. "Don't got no apples," the boy said, in a defensive tone. J did not reply to the boy. He only looked at him with a kind smile. At first, the boy avoided eye contact. Slowly, he raised his head, finally looking directly at J. Their eyes met. J's smile grew larger. It was infectious. The boy smiled back. It was as if a weight had been lifted from his shoulders.

"We don't have apples, but we do have carrots. Would you like me to give your ponies one?"

"That would be wonderful! Thank you so much," responded J. Those were the only words spoken between J and the boy. But it was enough to lessen the spell of the pandemic, at least temporarily.

On their way to the stables, they had passed the Golden Arch Inn. Walking back to it, they noticed suspicious stares from several of the villagers. One man in particular, standing just outside the stables, was watching them with dark and wary eyes. They ignored him and continued on their way to the Inn. J realized that this was the first time he had actually been inside a building in several days. He felt claustrophobic, which surprised him. He had never felt that way before. It was a small Inn, with only a few rooms and small dining area. The Innkeeper's wife stood behind the counter. She acted unfriendly and suspicious of strangers, a clear sign that she was afflicted by the pandemic. Fortunately, there were no men in the party, especially warriors, so she didn't perceive them as a threat.

"You'll be want-n' ah room, I suppose," she said, scowling at them. "Yes, please," sighed Rae, in a tired voice. It was apparent she needed food and a warm bed as soon as possible.

"Yr chill-ins?" the Innkeeper's wife asked.

"I am their Governess and can't wait to get them home," Rae replied, with a long weary sigh.

"Ur room tis top o-stairs, ta da right. Ma da-ter will make up da beds. Dinner tis red-dy if ur like-n' beef stew. Else, ur gon-na wait and pay extra."

"Beef stew is fine," Rae said. J licked his lips. He was more than ready to eat.

They deposited their bags in the room, then went down to dinner. At the bottom of the stairs, Raven saw the Innkeeper's daughter, carrying an armload of bedding.

"Let me help you," Raven said to the girl, who appeared to be about the same age. The daughter glanced up warily at Raven, then muttered, "Don-na need no help." Raven insisted, "Sure you do," and took half the bedding from her. J and Rae continued on into the dining room. The Innkeeper's wife served them three bowls of beef stew, a loaf of bread, butter, and a pitcher of water. She put the food down on the table without a word and walked away.

When Raven and the girl went to the bedroom, she said, "Let me help you make the beds." The girl shot her a suspicious look but said nothing. A person infected with the disease views an offer to help as manipulation. As they made the beds, Raven said, "You have beautiful hair, you know." The girl could not help but smile. She did have beautiful chestnut hair with natural curls. Those words began the process of counteracting the plague. Raven said no more, letting her kind words sink into the daughter's mind. After a few minutes, the girl asked, "Do ya re-a-lly think ma' hair's beau-tee-ful?" Raven looked directly into her eyes, "Yes, I really do. You are a beautiful person. I can see it in your eyes." The girl smiled shyly and looked away. "Ya bess be gettin' ta' ur din-ner. Iffn' ya don-na wan-na be getting' me in da trouble." Raven agreed and left.

The daughter began to sing a lullaby as she finished making the beds. Here is what she sang:

There was a young girl
Lovely and sweet
Beautiful from
Her head to her feet
When evil came
And the world was dark
She would shine
And sing like a lark
Her words were
A Glorious treat
Evil tried
But could not beat
The beautiful girl
Lovely and sweet

J was on his second helping of stew when Raven returned. She and Rae exchanged quick glances. Rae sensed that something had just happened with the daughter. "Did you speak to her?" Rae asked. "I only told her she was beautiful," Raven said, as she brought a spoonful of stew to her mouth.

After they finished the stew, the daughter served apple pie for dessert. Rae saw a smile on the girl's face, and knew Raven had successfully reversed the course of the plague within her. Rae was not the only person to witness the change. The man who had been at the stables earlier, seated now at a small table behind a pillar, also noticed. None of the three noticed him. He continued to watch, with a mysterious look on his face. Had any one of them seen him, they might have been frightened.

After J had a second piece of pie, they went up to their room. It did not take long for J to fall into a deep sleep. It was the first bed he had slept in for quite some time. Rae and Raven stayed up and spoke quietly to each other. They shared impressions of their travels thus far, and what challenges might lie ahead. Both wondered anxiously exactly how they would be able to vanquish evil. Finally, sleep came upon them too.

Deep in the night, the sound of heavy footsteps woke Raven. She lay very still, listening intently. They came closer to the door, then stopped. Her body stiffened when she heard the doorknob rattle. "Thankfully," she thought, "Rae locked the door." After a few moments, the footsteps retreated down the stairs.

"Rae, Rae!" Raven whispered, shaking her. "Did you hear that?"

"Yes, I did," replied Rae, reaching for the knife she kept under her pillow. No one knew she carried a knife. It was her secret weapon. For half an hour, the two listened without moving or making a sound. But the only sound they heard was J's deep breathing.

The sun was shining brightly the next morning. There was a warm breeze in the air, making it feel like spring. At breakfast, the daughter was happy to see them, and brought them warm porridge with maple syrup. "It'l stick to ur ribs," said the daughter. "By the way, my name is Naomi." J almost fell out of his chair. Naomi! He grinned from ear to ear. "You like my name?" she asked. "More than you know," J exclaimed, unable to contain his excitement.

The mysterious man was sitting at the same table as on the previous night. He was observing, making mental notes. This time, Rae noticed him. She whispered to the others, "Don't look now, but the man behind the pillar is staring at us." Raven suddenly got up and walked over to him. Although she was a force and very strong-willed, this was out of character even for her. Peering directly into the man's eyes, she said, "You find us interesting?"

His answer surprised her. "Best we not speak here. Also, it is better I am not seen with you. Meet me behind the stables in an hour." Raven did not say a word. She turned and went back to the table. "What was that all about?" J asked. "I am not sure," she answered. "He wants to meet us behind the stables in an hour."

They finished their breakfast, packed their things, and headed out. Much to their surprise, Naomi met them at the front door. She was beaming. Her smile went from ear to ear. "I made you a little treat." She handed J a basket. "Thank you. You are very kind," said J, taking the basket and smiling at her. He knew if it were "Naomi" food, it would be tasty. They were heartened by the change in Naomi. It seemed that the pandemic's antidote was beginning to work.

They arrived at the stables without incident. Villagers mostly ignored them. This was a good sign. The pandemic was losing its grip. The stable boy greeted them with a smile. Another good sign.

"Please saddle our ponies," requested Rae. "We will leave shortly. First, however, there is something we must do." The boy nodded and smiled, as if he knew they were about to meet the strange man. They made their way through the barn and exited out the back door. Looking to see if they were noticed, which they were not, Rae spoke softly, "We are here. What do you want?." As she spoke, her hand slipped around the hilt of her knife. It is always best to be prepared for danger. The man stepped out of a small wooden shed behind the stable. "Come in here," he whispered, gesturing with his hands to follow him. They were hesitant. If this were a trap, they would have no escape, once inside. "Quickly, before you are seen!," his voice sounding urgent. Looking at each other, they decided to follow the man. Rae gripped the knife handle with firm resolve. They stepped inside the building.

"You are in danger," he said, in a serious voice. "I cannot be seen with you," he continued. "It is not safe for any of us."

"Why?" asked J, who had figured the man was the only danger.

"Your speaking to the stable boy and Naomi has not gone unnoticed," he replied. "Evil is watching."

J spoke first, "I don't see any evil. The only person watching is you." Raven continued ,"Who else is watching? And who are YOU?"

"Who I am is not important. Evil knows you are coming. It is looking for you as we speak. Attempting to heal the boy and Naomi was a big mistake."

It was Rae's turn to ask, "How does evil know we are coming? No one has seen us here until yesterday."

"Evil does not know you are here, in the village. It only knows you will come, at some point, to annihilate it."

"How does it know that?" all three asked at the same time.

"It was foretold, at the time of the Great Queen, that evil would be driven out of the Middle World."

The man spoke boldly, with authority and conviction. He continued,

> You know about Matakwa, but you don't know about the "Circle of Six." You know that Matakwa, long ago, vanquished the pandemic, driving it out of *her* and the neighboring Kingdom. What you don't know is that the pandemic was not *completely* eradicated. It lurked in dark places, hiding, waiting for a chance to return. It was foretold that evil would return. The "Circle of Six" would drive it out of the Middle World forever!"

"Hmmm," wondered J. "We are only five. The Fellowship of Five."

"That was true when you left the cave," answered the man. "However, as Raven has observed in the Moon Pool, your party would become the "Circle of Six." It would take all six to drive evil from our world."

"How do you know all this?" asked Rae.

"I have studied manuscripts, all that I could find, for many years. My life has been devoted to scouring the cellars of palaces, searching for documents and writings about evil, and, in particular, its manifestation as a pandemic. My research has led me to this village, where I would find you."

Rae looked at Raven with alarm and concern. "Could this be the 'wise man'?" she wondered. "How do we know you are not evil in disguise?"

"If you believe that to be true, take your knife and slay me," said the man, as he knelt before Rae, offering his exposed neck to her knife. She drew her knife from its sheath. J reached out to stay Rae's hand. "No," he warned. "I believe this man."

"What else do you know?" J asked him.

"It was foretold that the Circle of Six would consist of a wizard, warrior, boy, girl, wise woman, and a wise man. I assume you two are the boy and girl," he said, looking at J and Raven. "And, you are the wise woman," pointing to Rae, "and the wizard and warrior must still be in the woods."

"So," said Raven, "does this mean you are the wise man?"

"Yes," he replied. "I have had visions of this meeting. I have been waiting in this village for several moons for your arrival."

"Well, if you are destined to join our company, what is your name?" asked Raven.

"I am Jackson from the Kingdom of Ra-tan, go-gan, me-can, su-lan and Maxfield. You can call me Jack. That's shorter."

"Well then, JACK," Raven added, emphasizing his name, "you will have to have the approval of Alvar, "the wizard," and Ranger, "the warrior," before you can join our company." Jack smiled. He had met Alvar long ago. They had been searching archives in Kambuka when they met. Both were looking for ancient tales of evil and pandemics. "How will I find them?" Jack asked. "It is not safe for me to ride out of the village with you."

"Ride east towards the next village. We will find you," said Rae, who had started to take a liking to Jack. Her eyes betrayed the attraction.

The trio returned to the stables, where the boy had saddled the ponies and gave extra carrots to J for them. Jack remained in the shed long after the party departed. When it was safe, he had the stable boy saddle his pony and he rode east, in the opposite direction of the party. He took a slow ride out of town. After traveling a few leagues, he found a place to wait, which was secluded and next to a stream. An avid reader, Jack took an ancient manuscript from his saddlebag. He read, waiting for the Fellowship of Five. It was early afternoon when they arrived.

"Hello, Jack," the Wizard said. Jack stood up, "Good to see you again," he replied. "I believe it was in the archive cellar of Kambuka that we last met," said the Wizard. "Tell us what you have done since."

Jack recounted how the archives had foretold of evil's return, in the form of a pandemic. During the times of both the Great Queen and Matakwa, evil had come from across the sea. It had spread to the eastern shore of the Middle World. So, he traveled east, searching archives. His travels led him to all the kingdoms between Zarlaka (Ponakwa's home), Kambuka (J's home), and the eastern shore. In each kingdom, he studied the archives to find out all he could about the pandemic. Many of the archives were partially destroyed, due to time, water, fire, and wars. But with diligence, he was able to piece together how the pandemic spread. More importantly, he learned how to stop it.

"How can it be stopped?" asked J.

"You and Raven will stop it," answered Jack. "I discovered the prophecy of Cal-a-man-dough. Cal-a-man-dough was a tiny kingdom nestled high in the Silver Mountains. It was deserted long ago due to famine. I found the remains of the palace. Deep in the tombs, I discovered the prophecy."

"What was the prophecy?" asked J.

That evil would return. As before, it would infect the eastern shore with a terrible plague. Many people would die. Then, it would spread west. The next few pages were burned and smudged. I was able to pick out only a word here and there. The words I found were, Beauty and Grace. After more years of searching, I finally figured out what the words meant. But then, you already know what they mean. After all, the five of you are here.

"Why are you telling us something we already know?" asked Ranger, who was standing guard for the troupe.

"Because there are six in the Circle. You make five." answered Jack.

"I see," muttered Ranger, "and you are the sixth?"

"Only if you wish it to be so. I have traveled all the lands between here and the shore. I know many ways to get there. Also, the path to the Silver Mountain is dangerous. You will need a guide."

"In that case," said Rae, "I think Jack should complete the Circle of Six."

The others agreed. The Circle was now complete.

James Black

Chapter 6

Winston and Watermelon

It was decided that Jack should go to the next village first. Rae, J, Winston, and Raven would follow a few hours later. Alvar and Ranger would stay out of sight. J felt sorry for them. They would have to spend another night outside, eating cold food and sleeping on the hard ground. For them, however, it was not a hardship. They had grown accustomed to living in the outdoors.

Jack knew the village, having visited it many times before. He had scouted it out, as well as many of the other villages between Alvar's cave and the eastern shore. His plan, after learning of the events to come, was to serve as the Circle's guide. This necessitated that he be familiar with the roads, villages, and people they would encounter on their quest. Upon entering the new village, named Wilsonville, he made his way to the stables. As he rode through the town, he carefully scanned the villagers' faces. Most of them already knew him, so their stares would give him a good indication of the extent to which the pandemic was present. Jack saw right away that it was worse than the last village. But the situation was not hopeless. J and Raven would have enough Beauty and Grace to turn the tide of the epidemic there.

After bedding his horse (Jack rode a gray mare instead of a pony), he walked up Main Street to the Bucking Bronco Inn. Paintings and sculptures of horses adorned the Inn's interior. Jack was aware of the Innkeeper's affinity for horses. He arranged for a room, then found a corner table in the dining room where he could see, but not be seen.

J, Rae, and Raven went directly to the Bucking Bronco, as Jack had instructed them to do. They also took Winston. Mules were a novelty in Wilsonville. This would give the trio a topic to discuss with the Innkeeper. Winston did not like being a "novelty." He let his disgust be known with several snorts and stomps. Nevertheless, he went along with the plan and agreed to play his part. As they rode up, the Innkeeper came out to see the mule.

"Be that-ta mu-ell?" asked the gray-haired and bearded Innkeeper.

"It is," replied Rae. Winston swished his tail, snorted and stomped, again expressing his disgust.

The Innkeeper approached Winston to take a closer look and touched him.

"Careful," said J. "He bites."

"Wont-ta be ah bite-in' meeee. I knowsss how ta handle dem beasties," he replied. Winston could have turned his head towards the Innkeeper, bitten him, and turned away before he knew what happened. Beauty and Grace, however, prevailed. The old bearded man was spared that pain and humiliation. Reaching out to touch Winston, however, was too much for the mule to bear. With a quick turn of his rump, his tail swished the man across the face. Trying to ignore the pain, he said, "Looks like dat dang mueeeel needsa less-on in behavin'." Raven hurried up to the Innkeeper and asked,

"Are you hurt?" her hand gently stroking his face. Her words and her touch had an immediate effect. He looked into her eyes as if a change had just come over him.

"It did sting a little. But you made it feel much better. Thank you," he said with gratitude.

As they watched Winston, the town Mayor marched up. He was wearing a black three-piece suit with a gold watch chain hanging from his vest. He was in his early 60's and it was apparent time had not been kind to him. His wrinkled skin, gray beard, and bent back, gave him the appearance of a man who had lived a difficult life. It was also clear to the travelers that the Mayor had a severe case of the virus.

"Who are these people and what are they doing in MY town?" The Mayor demanded an answer from the Innkeeper.

"They just arrived, Your Honor. I don't know who they are," the Innkeeper answered.

"Who are you?!" again demanded the Mayor. This time he directed the question to Rae.

"Your Honor," she replied, "we wish only to rest here for the night." She wanted to add that they were traveling east, but thought better of it.

"Well, you best be on your way by sunup tomorrow morning. We don't like strangers with peculiar ideas here. My town is safe. I mean to keep it that way. Do you understand?!"

Rae understood. She also could see how devastating the effects of the pandemic could be. Both J and Raven understood and thought to themselves, "If the virus is this bad way out here, how terrible it must be on the eastern shore."

"Your Honor," Rae replied, "we mean no harm and will be gone early tomorrow morning."

The Mayor turned with a loud grunt and stomped away. No one spoke for a few moments. The Innkeeper went inside. The party took their ponies down to the livery stable, then walked back to the Bucking Bronco. As they did, they kept their eyes down, only glancing up briefly to steal a quick peek at the faces of the villagers staring at them. They could tell they were not welcome. The plague had taken its toll here, for sure.

Back at the Bucking Bronco, they were given a small room, again at the top of the stairs. This time, there was no girl with bed sheets. The room was already prepared. So, they went down to eat. The food was cold and bland. Not much better than what the Wizard and Ranger would probably be eating. A warm fire was the only inviting aspect of the dining room. After dining, the three huddled around the fireplace. Sitting off to the side was an older man, also bearded, smoking a pipe.

"Your pipe's aroma is lovely," said Raven. "What is it you are smoking?"

"Tobacco of the whisper leaf," he replied. "We are known for our fine tobacco."

"It does smell wonderful," Raven said, with a sweet smile. She could see her words were affecting the old man.

"I have been here all my life. My tobacco farm is just south of town. We have been growing tobacco for generations," he added, with a slight smile. Raven could see he was proud of his farm and its crops.

"Do you grow other things too?" Raven asked, seeking to continue the conversation.

"Oh yes," he replied. "We have large gardens and orchards with fruit and vegetables. Our specialty is watermelon."

At the sound of watermelon, J perked up. "I love watermelon," he said, licking his lips. The old man smiled at the thought of seeing J eat his watermelon.

"On your way out tomorrow morning, stop by my farm. I will give you a taste," he said.

J and Raven could see their Beauty and Grace were affecting the old farmer. However, they were careful not to speak too long with him. The Mayor would certainly notice. That was something they did not want to have happen, for the virus would cause the Mayor to do bad things. So, they ended the conversation and went to their room.

Jack, who had been watching, ambled over to the farmer. "Would it be possible for me to purchase a pouch of your fine tobacco?" he asked. "Sure, Jack," he replied. "Come by tomorrow. I will set aside a pouch of my best leaf for you."

The next day, Rae, Raven, and J left early, as ordered by the Mayor. The Innkeeper walked with them down to the livery stable. He wanted to see the mule one more time. Winston had been groomed, fed grain, and a delicious apple. He was in the best mood possible, for a mule. When they arrived, he brayed a hearty welcome.

The Innkeeper cautiously approached Winston. J said to Winston, "This is our friend. He wants to pet you." Winston did not reply. Although animals can speak, they only do that in Kambuka. They never speak in other kingdoms. Winston stood still and let the Innkeeper stroke his neck. A giant smile spread across his face.

"I have never touched a mule before," he beamed.

"Winston is very special to us," replied J, with an equally large smile on his face. Beauty and Grace. The Innkeeper was being cured.

They rode south before the sun rose. Upsetting the Mayor was not in their plans. Riding to the watermelon farm was. Especially for J. It was a short distance away. Upon their arrival, the farmer was waiting for them. "How did you know what time we would be here?" asked J.

"The Mayor is very strict about travelers leaving before dawn. Come, try some fresh watermelon." J did not need a second invitation. He followed the farmer inside and sat down at the kitchen table. There, on a plate, was a giant slice of fresh watermelon. J's eyes lit up and a smile filled his face as he took a bite. It was sweet and juicy. He ate the whole slice without stopping to take a breath.

"This is the best watermelon I have ever had!" J exclaimed. The expression on his face emanated Beauty and Grace. The farmer felt J's words were spoken sincerely. "Thank you," he replied.

"I am afraid we must be going," said Rae, with an air of disappointment that they could not stay and eat more. Knowing the Mayor would send spies out, they did not want to get the farmer in trouble. The farmer gave them a freshly picked watermelon to take with them. The travelers thanked him. They were surprised to hear the farmer say,

"It is I that thank YOU!" Nothing further was said, but it was plain to see he was cured.

They had been gone about an hour when Jack arrived at the farm. His intent was to see the effects of Raven and J on the farmer. Jack was greeted by a smiling and happy farmer. "Here, take two pouches," he said. That was all Jack needed to hear.

Chapter 8

Glamdor, Master of Glamring

"Between Wilsonville and the Silver Mountains, there are only a few small villages. Because they are not on the East-West road, there are very few villagers infected with the pandemic. There is very little contact with outsiders. The danger from here to the Silver Mountains comes from bandits. There are three gangs that control different sections of the East-West road. They are bad men. To add to that, they are also infected. This makes them doubly dangerous. We could avoid the road, which would add a fortnight to our journey," explained Jack.

"How large are these gangs of highwaymen?" asked the Wizard. "There are only six to ten members in each gang. However, they know the best places to ambush travelers, and are quite willing to inflict harm," answered Jack.

"We will need a strategy," said Ranger, with an air of authority. "A strategy that capitalizes on our strengths."

"What are our strengths?" asked J.

"Our greatest strengths are Beauty and Grace," said Ranger. "Our strategy must be built on them. I suggest we start with J. The highwaymen will not perceive him as a threat or someone to rob."

J was immediately gripped with fear. He did not like this strategy at all. "What could I do?" he asked. "I am only a young boy."

"You must go into their camp and make friends with the leader," instructed Ranger. "Use your guile."

It was agreed that Ranger and J would go ahead of the troupe and seek out the gangs. This would require them to go on foot through the forest with stealth. Their plan was for J to sneak into the highwaymen's camp unnoticed. Then present himself. The others would camp out of sight for three days, then head east on the East-West road.

Ranger had no time to train J for what was ahead. The pandemic would not wait that long. So, they left right away. Earlier that morning, J had been enjoying watermelon at the farmer's table. Now he was trudging down the East-West road on an empty stomach. To make matters worse, it began to rain. Ranger said the rain was a blessing. It would keep the highwaymen in their camps and not out on the road. Being in camp meant J could join them under the pretext of getting out of the rain.

"Together," Ranger said to J, "we will find the closest gang's camp. You will walk in and tell them you are lost. That you are wet and hungry. And you wish to join them. Use your guile to convince them.

Once they take you in, begin to slowly show your Beauty and Grace. These are bandits and robbers. They are villains and thugs. The Beauty and Grace you show them must be different. Saying their hair is beautiful, as Raven said to Naomi, will not work. You must speak in the language of the outlaw."

J's mind was conflicted. Fear told him to run back home to Kambuka. "Flee while you still can. Wait until Ranger sleeps. Then, sneak out and run as fast and far as you can," fear whispered to his mind. There was another part of his mind counseling him differently:

You were chosen to save the Middle World. It is your destiny. You cannot abandon the Circle and let the Middle World succumb to the virus.

He recognized these words as the truth. "No," he thought, "I shall not abandon my destiny." Although fear never left his mind, he resolved to follow his path as the Chosen One and do what he knew needed to be done.

It did not take Ranger long to find the first camp. Highwaymen are not very good at covering their tracks. There was a guard posted at the camp entrance. However, he was wearing a poncho which kept him dry, but his head was buried in the hood which prevented him from seeing anyone approaching.

"The camp is just ahead," whispered Ranger. "Walk in as if you are lost and hungry. Tell them you have come to join their gang and were willing to walk through the rain to find them."

J did just that. His walk was more of a stumble as he came into the camp. At first, the gang did not see him. When they did, their response was to laugh at him. "What have we here?" one of the bandits yelled. "A lost boy," said another. The ruffians teased J and jostled him back and forth. This went on for a few minutes until the leader said, "Stop. What are you doing here in the middle of the night?" This was J's moment of truth. If he said the wrong thing, he could be killed. Taking a deep breath, he said, "I want to be a highwayman. I have come to join your gang."

"You are a mere boy. We don't take boys, only men," said the leader, whose name was Timmon.

"True, I am a boy," J spoke confidently, "But I found your camp, and sneaked in without being noticed. I have many other strengths too."

Timmon rubbed his chin and considered J's words. It was true, he did find the camp and sneak in unnoticed. That could prove valuable to the gang. "What other strengths do you have?" asked Timmon.

Without hesitation, J replied, "Beauty and Grace."

The bandits broke out in uproarious laughter. "That's ridiculous," cried one of the bandits between bouts of laughter.

"It is not!" exclaimed J. "Each of you has been infected with a virus, the pandemic, evil. I can cure you."

These words brought the laughter to a halt. "Pandemic?" Timmon asked. "What virus, pandemic? What are you talking about?"

J continued, "When you set out to rob a traveler, are you all of one mind? Or do you argue among yourselves? Do you sometimes harm travelers for no reason?"

"So what if we do? We are highwaymen."

"That is true. You are highwaymen. But if you cause too much harm, or injure or kill travelers, the King will send his soldiers. You will be arrested and jailed. Perhaps even hanged. And, I must point out, you are not very good at hiding. If a boy can sneak into your camp so easily, just think what soldiers could do."

Those words struck a chord with Timmon. J's Beauty and Grace began to reverse the course of the virus in the gang.

"Feed the boy," he instructed. "He will stay in my tent tonight." J found the tent comfortable. Once settled in and wrapped up in warm blankets, he began to talk with Timmon. He was tempted to suggest that the gang stop robbing travelers. However, the nature of a person is never something easily changed. Highwaymen are robbers by trade. That is their nature. Nevertheless, J decided to follow the path of Beauty and Grace.

"You know," J said, "robbing is your nature. As it is for the other gangs on the East-West road. Like I said before, too much robbing, maiming, and killing will bring the King's soldiers down on you. Even if your gang only robs, and the other gangs continue their ways, you will suffer the consequences. Perhaps you could form a Union with the other gangs. Agree to rob travelers only once and share the spoils. You could even call it a toll for using the road. If your gangs kept the road in good repair, travelers would be willing to pay even more."

The leader thought long and hard about J's words as the boy slept. The next morning, J woke to the sounds of men preparing to leave. He watched as they followed Timmon out of the camp. Only two guards were left behind. "Where are they going?" asked J. "To a parley," replied the taller of the guards. "What is a parley?" asked J. "It is a temporary truce when gang leaders meet to talk. Timmon has gone to meet with the other gangs to talk about your idea of a toll."

J thought to himself, "My work here is done." He told the guards he had decided being a highwayman was not for him. He wished them well and departed. He was only a short way from the camp when Ranger appeared. "How did you fare?"

"Very well!" J said, with an infectious smile. "Guile works WELL!."

On their way back to Alvar, Raven, and Rae, J told Ranger what had happened. How he had spoken with Timmon and of the ensuing parley. Ranger was amazed at J's resourcefulness. It was true, J WAS the Chosen One. When they arrived back at the camp, Ranger told the troupe they could now travel the East-West road. Depending on the outcome of the parley, the road might or might not be safe to travel. There would be a toll, regardless of the parley's outcome. Raven wanted to know all about J's experience at the gang's camp. She listened carefully as J told her how he had spoken with Timmon. While J was telling his tale, the Wizard took Ranger aside. They spoke in hushed tones. After J finished the conversation, the Wizard summoned him over.

"J," he said, "do you remember asking me to teach you how to use a sword? Do you remember what I recommended you needed to learn first?"

J's memory was hazy. It had something to do with Grace. The word "not" was also vaguely in his memory.

"I told you that you first needed to learn about Beauty and Grace. Next, how NOT to use a sword.

After that, you could begin your sword training. You have successfully demonstrated Beauty and Grace at the highwaymen's camp. You did that without a sword. It is time you begin your sword training." The Wizard reached into his pack and took out a small sword in an ornate leather scabbard. The handle was T-shaped, with ancient runes inscribed in both the handle and blade. He handed the sword to J.

"This is yours now. It was forged in the furnaces of the Great Queen. The iron forger, named Wallsea, infused it with magic and power and named it Glamring, which means 'evil slayer'. It had been prophesized that a boy and girl would be chosen to drive evil out of the Middle World. In that prophecy, the boy would wield Glamring, with all its magic and power, to save the Middle World."

"That boy is you, J," said Alvar. "You are the Chosen One." With that, he handed the sword to J, who accepted it with reverence and awe. He was beginning to understand his destiny.

"The magic and power of Glamring is only for you, J. The runes inscribed on the blade state, 'He who wields this sword shall be called **Glamdor, Master of Glamring**'. No one else can access its power. It is a sacred weapon. You must use it only in the commission of your destiny." J held the sword up and drew circles in the air with it.

"It is light as a feather," J told the Wizard.

"Yet it has the power of lightning and the force of a great hammer," replied Alvar. Soon J would find out just how powerful Glamring really was.

The Circle made their way to the East-West road. J and Raven were in the lead. They were several hundred yards ahead of the others. Highwaymen, who might be lying in wait, were more likely to consider the two as innocent children, rather than armed adults. Since J was known by Timmon's gang, they would likely be friendly. In the event of serious trouble, Ranger and the Wizard could rush to their aid. Rae and Jack would serve as back-up protection.

They rode several leagues, passing Timmon's section of the road without incident. Apparently, Timmon had not had enough time to return from the parley and set up an ambush for travelers. As they entered the next section of the road, Raven heard the birds singing a warning song. She hesitated, signaling for J to stop and listen. J's hand reached for the hilt of Glamring. He felt its power and himself changing, becoming powerful. Raven sang her friendship song. The birds responded, signaling that men were hiding around the next bend in the road. Raven sang something J did not understand. A small chickadee flew off to the west. Raven whispered the news to J. They reined in their ponies to a slow walk, as they approached the bend. On either side of the road, the banks rose, leaving the travelers in a gully and vulnerable. After rounding the bend, they were confronted with highwaymen high up on both banks. Some had bows and arrows, drawn and aimed at J and Raven. Their leader, named Tammon, stepped out from behind a tree. Apparently, in this part of the East-West road, gang leaders had similar names. Only the second letter was different (Timmon and Tammon).

"What do we have here"? said Tammon. J had heard the same words before when he entered Timmon's camp.

"We do not wish any trouble," said J with kindness and authority. "We come from Timmon's camp. I am traveling under his protection. I know of the parley." Tammon was silent for a moment, then said, "You may pass." J went on to say, "We have traveling companions following behind us. They are under Timmon's protection also."

"Why are you not all traveling together?" asked Tammon.

"We did not want to appear hostile. Our company includes a warrior and wizard," J replied. "Also, there are a man and woman."

At that moment, the four remining members of the Circle arrived. Raven had sent the chickadee to warn the company. They rode with haste to protect J and Raven. When they arrived, they found no need for protection. Tammon waved them on. They passed without incident and rode several more leagues without encountering another person. When they stopped for lunch, the Raven told the company how J had dealt with Tammon. How his word had been spoken with confidence and authority she had never seen in J before. He was becoming Glamdor, although she did not realize it. It his Grace she saw.

After lunch, the Circle took up the same travel pattern. J and Raven rode ahead once again. It was midafternoon when they entered the last gang's section of the road. This gang was led by Tommon. As before, Raven listened for warning songs. When she heard them, she sang back to the birds her song of friendship. The birds warned her of danger ahead. Highwaymen were hiding in the forest. This time, Raven sent a blue jay to the Wizard. They approached with caution. There was no bend. Rather, the road ran straight through deep woods. This could prove to be a problem because the highwaymen could see the Circle coming to J and Raven's rescue.

Men jumped out from the forest on both sides of the road, encircling Raven and J. For the third time, J heard, "What do we have here?" As before, J said, "We come from Timmon's camp. I am traveling under his protection. I know of the parley." This time, things were different.

"So, you think that will protect you?" barked Tommon. "Well, you are mistaken, boy! I made no deal with Timmon. Being from his camp makes you a mortal enemy."

This was not what J had expected. His hand reached for Glamring. "I would not do that if I were you, boy!" said Tommon. J looked left and right, seeing Tommon's gang also reaching for their swords. Much to his surprise, Glamring's magic flung J off his horse, and lunged at Tommon's neck, before he could react. J spoke, not as J, but as Glamdor, "Call off your ruffians or I will free your body from your head." He spoke loudly enough for the entire gang to hear.

"You heard him!" cried Tommon, fearing for his life, "Put your weapons away!"

At that moment, the company rode up. They saw Glamdor holding Glamring poised to sever Tommon's head.

Glamdor spoke again, "We will take Tommon with us, for a few leagues. At the first sign of trouble, Glamring will send him into the next life. Is that clear?"

Tommon, in a resigned and fearful tone, said, "Yes, yes, it is clear. Please don't kill me! There will be no trouble."

The Circle slowly left the woods. Tommon walked at the head of the company. Glamdor was right behind him ready to use Glamring.

It was two leagues before the Circle left the woods, entering into an open plain. Tommon was released. He ran as fast as he could back to his gang, not wanting to be with the Circle for a moment longer than necessary.

J had entered the woods as a boy. He emerged as **Glamdor, Master of Glamring**, the Chosen One. It would take both time and dangerous encounters to fully realize his potential. Nevertheless, J was no longer the same boy. His life would be changed forever.

James Black

Chapter 9

A Time to Reflect

The Circle emerged from the woods and had their first glimpse of the Silver Mountains. Between them and the mountains stretched the vast Golden Plains. It derived that name by virtue of its rich agriculture. Wheat, oats, corn, barley, and a variety of other crops flourished. Food was always plentiful. What they could not see was the Great Rift Depression, miles and miles of swamps, forests of tangled vines, and unnatural creatures. Alvar and Jack knew all about the Depression but chose not to tell the others. They wanted to give the Circle time to rest and regain their strength.

Jack suggested they spend the night at an Inn he was familiar with that was a short distance north of the East-West road. He had stayed there before, on his way to Wilsonville. It was very likely the company would be the only guests, and the Innkeeper was known for protecting the privacy of his guests. After spending many nights in the outdoors, Alvar and Ranger were especially keen on having a warm bath and sleeping in a bed.

They arrived at the Inn after dark. Jack secured rooms for the Circle. Rae and Raven shared one room, Jack and J, another, and Alvar and Ranger, the third. After settling in, they met in the dining room for dinner. A long table had been set with three place settings on each side. A flagon of beer, carafe of wine, and large pitcher of cold apple cider were already there, along with warm rolls, freshly churned butter, and honey. For the first time in a long time, the Circle enjoyed a good meal together. Alvar, who loved beer, took a deep draught, causing beer to run down his beard. A rare smile grew on his face.

"My dear traveling companions," he began, "you have been through much and deserve a rest." Being a wizard, he himself could not enjoy the moment. When on a quest, wizards never stop to "smell the roses". He wanted the others to enjoy what he could not. Unfortunately, the next words out of his mouth had the opposite effect. He continued, "The worst is yet to come. I only hope you are all up to the task."

That is a problem with wizards. Even when they try to be helpful and kind, it often backfires.

Rae and Jack, who were drinking wine, did not let Alvar's comments spoil their cheerful mood. Jack stood up and announced,

"A toast to our young companions, Raven and Glamdor, formally our boy, J. They may be the youngest of our company, but they certainly are not the least important."

"Here, here," said Rae and Ranger in agreement.

J, who had just finished his second roll with butter and honey, also chimed in with a toast, "To the Innkeeper, who makes the best rolls in all of the Middle World." All of a sudden, J's tone of voice sounded deeper and more confident. He was in the process of transitioning to Glamdor.

The evening progressed with merriment and wonderful food. Even Winston, who spent the evening in the stable, was groomed, fed grain and fresh carrots. He too enjoyed the time to rest. By the end of the meal, everyone was ready for bed, except Rae. She was looking forward to a long hot bath. Soaking in the water, with lots of mineral salts and essential oils, she felt like a queen. Following her bath, she retired to her room. Raven was already sound asleep. To her surprise, Jack was waiting there with a champagne bottle.

"I thought you might like a nightcap," he whispered, not wanting to wake Raven. "Wonderful," her voice was soft and relaxed. This was the first time they had spent quiet moments together. It seemed natural, and before long they were sharing funny stories about their lives. Jack shared the story about when he had gone days without a bath. His travels took him by a river, where he jumped in, naked. As luck would have it, no sooner had he gone in the water than a stagecoach suddenly arrived. It had stopped to give the passengers a rest. Upstream was a shallow place with waterlilies, where he hid until the stagecoach left.

Rae and Jack formed a bond that night that lasted all the rest of their lives.

The troupe stayed the following day at the Inn. They relaxed, enjoyed good food, and laughed together. They told stories about their life experiences. Rae told the story about the knife she carried. When she was Raven's age, there was a hunting contest. It was for boys only. The boy who bagged the biggest animal would win the prize. The prize, as you might guess, was the knife that Rae ultimately carried. She was going to compete and had no intention of letting the fact that she was a girl hinder her. She cut her hair short, put on boy clothes, and went to the registration tent in the village's main square. The tent was full of old hunters with long beards.

"I wish to enter the hunting contest," Rae said. They looked her over. "You look too young to compete," said a gruff old hunter.

"Where does it say there is an age or size limit?" retorted Rae.

"Sign here," said the hunter running the contest. She signed her name not as Rae, but Alwin, the male version of her name.

"Wait over there with the other boys," said the old man, pointing to a group of boys with bows and arrows. Some had long bows, while others had short, recurved bows. Rae did not have a bow. She only had a rope. The other boys laughed at her for not having a "proper" hunting bow. One boy, the oldest and biggest, was especially mean to her, calling her a sissy who was too small to handle a bow and arrow.

"We shall see," responded Rae.

"Listen up!" yelled the old hunter, getting the boys' attention. "The contest rules are as follows: you have until sundown to hunt. The boy who returns with the biggest catch wins the Hunter's Knife," which he held up for all to see.

"I'll win," said the biggest and oldest boy. As before, Rae responded, "We shall see."

"The hunt begins NOW!" shouted the old hunter.

The boys scrambled off in all directions. Running as fast as they could, to find and shoot the biggest animal they could find. Rae hesitated. She waited until all the boys were gone. The old hunter came up to her, asking,

"What is the matter? Are you not going? Are you afraid? Is hunting too difficult for you?"

"Not afraid," replied Rae, "waiting for just the right moment to begin tracking my prey."

The old man shook his head with a confused look and walked away. Rae watched him leave, then headed into the woods. She heard the boys calling to each other. She was listening for the oldest boy, who had teased her. After an hour or so, one of the boys yelled,

"I shot a turkey! A wild turkey!"

Rae ignored him, continuing to track the oldest boy. During the day, other boys shot pheasants and partridges. Squirrels and even a raccoon were shot. Many of the boys, including Rae's prey, climbed up into trees, hoping animals would come walking by. When they did, they would be easy targets. Rae scouted around the area where the oldest boy was treed, making sure he did not see her. She set a trap for him. First, Rae found an old hickory tree with a large limb stretched over the path back to the village. She made a large noose at one end of her rope and placed it under the tree. Then, she covered it with leaves. Next, she strung the rope over the limb, then waited. It was late in the afternoon when Rae heard the oldest boy exclaim, "I shot a giant tom turkey!" She readied her rope and waited for him. He was full of himself, thinking he would certainly win. Not paying attention, he walked right into Rae's trap. As soon as he stepped into the noose, she sprang the trap. Holding the other end of the rope, she jumped from the tree. The noose tightened around the boy's ankles, then lifted him upside down into the air.

"Let me down!" he screamed. Rae, ignoring his screams, tied his hands behind his back with a small section of rope. Then, she tied another length about three feet long around his neck. Slowly she let him down.

"Ok," she said, "now we will return to the village." Upon returning, she presented her "catch" to the old hunter.

"What is this?" he asked. "My catch," she replied. "I am here to claim my prize."

Rae had not only captured the boy, she also had his turkey. The old man had no choice but to award her the prize. So, with some reluctance, he declared,

"Alwin is the winner. Alwin, here is your prize." He handed her the knife.

Rae took the knife from her belt. She held it up for all the Circle to see. J had a naughty thought. He decided, as a way to tease her, he would call her "Al".

"That was a lovely story, "Al", he said with a mischievous grin. Rae took a length of rope from her bag. "I would be careful if I were you," she said to J, with a twinkle in her eye.

James Black

Chapter 10

The Journey Continues

The Circle woke to a cold and wet day. Not a good omen. Some wanted to stay another day at the Inn. The food was good, and the fireplace was inviting. Alvar did not want to delay. Time was of the essence. The pandemic was spreading. So, after a filling breakfast, they set out. They made their way back to the East-West road. Looking to the east, they saw dark, menacing clouds. Unfortunately, they were riding into a storm. When the weather was fair, the Golden Plains could be beautiful. Traveling would be easy, without hills, valleys, or steep curves. Only an easy straight road to follow. On the other hand, when it rained, there was no place in which to take shelter.

The wind began to gain momentum. They had to bend into it as their ponies trudged forward. Then, it started to rain. At first it was light, like little pinpricks. Later it grew heavier, finally transforming into hail. They had to stop. The ponies stood side-by-side, with the travelers grouped in front of them. One wonderful thing about horses, ponies, and mules, is that they know how to withstand wind and hail. They stand with their rumps facing the wind, protecting their heads. The troupe huddled in front of the animals, who were blocking the wind. The cold, however, was getting worse. Even though they all were wearing their warmest clothes, they still began to shiver. They knew if they stayed there, they could freeze to death. If they left, they might get lost in the storm and freeze. At the moment when things looked the bleakest, J's hand brushed against the hilt of Glamring. It felt warm. He wrapped his hand around the hilt. Even warmer. He drew Glamring from its sheath. The blade was warm, glowing bright red. J felt his whole body warming. Glamdor was emerging from within him.

"Form a circle," Glamdor instructed the troupe. He held the hilt and placed Glamring's tip in the snow. Immediately, the company felt its emanating warmth. In only a few minutes, they were feeling better. Glamdor shoved the tip into the ground and let go of the hilt. The sword began to cool. He touched the hilt, causing the heat to return.

"There is an old tale," Alvar ruminated out loud, "about a man named Mosswell. He lived in the kingdom of E-got-naught. He and his family were not originally from E-got-naught, but had fled there to escape a famine. They were treated as outsiders and never liked. One day, Mosswell decided to take his family and leave E-got-naught. At first, the King was glad to see them go. No sooner had they started to leave, however, than the King changed his mind.

Mosswell's family were industrious workers. He couldn't afford to lose them. The King ordered his army to bring them back. Mosswell soon found himself trapped between a very large lake and the King's army. Mosswell had a magical staff, similar to Glamdor's magical Glamring. As he lifted his staff high above his head, the water began to part. In a short time, there was a dry path for Mosswell's family to follow. They made their way to the other side of the lake. No sooner had they made it to the other side, than the King's army arrived. The soldiers raced down into the path. Mosswell, seeing the army approaching his side of the lake, lowered his staff. The water rushed in, drowning all the soldiers."

Glamdor, whose hand was still gripping the sword, said, "I hope this storm doesn't last too long. My arm is getting tired." Raven scooched over next to him. She stretched out her arm and supported his wrist with her hand. "Do you remember what I told you at the Moon Pool?"

The storm lasted through most of the night. Other members of the troupe also helped Glamdor hold his arm and hand up. When dawn finally broke, the sky had cleared. The sun shone brightly. It wasn't long before the snow began to melt, which led to the next challenge. The East-West road had turned into thick mud, making travel difficult. They had to walk beside the road, which was covered with tall grasses.

That, too, was difficult to traverse. It was not until late afternoon that the road finally dried out.

Now that the road was passable, they decided to continue for an hour after dark, to make up for lost time. When they finally did stop, no fire was started. They ate cold food and went to sleep right away. Just before dawn, the grass began to rustle. Raven was the first to wake. She heard the rustling, which was strange. The wind was still. She sang to the birds, a song of warning. No reply. That too was strange. What she did not know was that the birds had all fled. Raven shook Ranger awake.

"Wake up!" she whispered. "Listen. What is that sound?"

"It sounds like grass rustling," his voice expressing concern. Ranger shook Alvar, who jumped up out of his sleep. He was standing tall, holding his staff. He sniffed the air. At that moment, Winston let out a fearful and deafening bray.

"RUN!" shouted Alvar. "Run for your LIFE!"

In a flash, the company was up. J began to roll up his blanket. "No time for THAT!" yelled Alvar, "run for your life!"

Without hesitation, the troupe mounted their ponies and rode east as fast as their mounts would carry them. Winston, who did not run fast, did his best to keep up. He knew what had caused the grass to rustle. It was the Grass People. He also knew that Grass People considered mule meat a delicacy.

Grass People live in grass huts which blend in with the grasses of the Golden Plain. The huts are invisible to the untrained eye. Their diet consists mainly of fruit and vegetables. Mule and horse meat are rare delicacies for them. The Circle did not know that the place they had chosen to spend the night was near one of the Grass Peoples' camp. Grass People do not reside in villages. They are nomads, who travel the Golden Plains in search of game. When they find a stream or small lake, they set up camp and wait. Being fierce hunters, they are able to sneak up and kill game effectively. Grass People hunt in large groups, encircling their prey, then close in for the kill. As a general rule, they also kill any humans they find. This keeps word spreading to other humans about their existence.

The scent of Winston and the ponies made its way to their camp. A hunting party of fifty Grass Men encircled the company. They were within a hundred yards when Winston brayed in alarm. There were three Grass Men on the East-West road. They were there in order to block any escapees. As the Circle approached, Glamdor yelled to them, "Let me by!" Drawing Glamring, he charged the trio. Glamring flashed bright as the sun, blinding the three Grass Men. They fell backwards off the road. The company charged through and galloped to safety. It was two leagues before they stopped. Winston was exhausted. The ponies were wet with lather. Even Jack's mare was dripping wet.

After resting, they took stock of their provisions. Most of them had been left behind. Fortunately, Ranger had insisted the company sleep in their clothes. They kept their boots close by so they could slip them on in a hurry. But, beyond the clothes on their backs, they had very little.

"We will have to replenish our provisions very soon," warned Jack. "The Golden Plains City is 12 leagues from here. We can get there by nightfall if we don't tarry."

"We have no money. It was left behind with our packs," commented Rae. "How will we buy supplies?"

"Don't worry. I will get money," replied Ranger. "How?" asked Rae. "Leave that to me," Ranger said, flashing a sly smile.

Very few words were spoken during the ride to The Golden Plains City. Most of the Circle were lost in their own thoughts. Narrowly escaping death was an extremely scary experience for all, except for Ranger and Alvar.

Entering a city was a dangerous risk for the Circle. Evil would have a better opportunity to discover their whereabouts, and devise ways to stop or even kill them. Unfortunately, they had no choice.

Their provisions were gone. Only Winston and the ponies would have been equipped to continue, being that the Golden Plains had all the food they would need.

"Too bad humans can't eat grass," muttered Winston. "We could travel much faster if we did not always have to stop and eat meals. All they would have to do is munch some grass and drink water from streams."

Humans are not grazing animals, so going into the city was necessary. Jack led them to an Inn on the outskirts of town, figuring there would be fewer guests and less of an opportunity for evil to find out they were there. Once settled in their rooms, Ranger announced he was going out and would return with money. "I hope so," said Rae. "We don't have money to pay for these rooms."

Ranger had been without money before, but he learned that he could make money playing cards. So, he found a saloon with several card tables, and joined one of the games. He had a few coins in his pants pocket, which got him started. One of Ranger's many talents was his ability to "read" people, especially when they were playing cards. By looking at their expressions, he could tell if they were holding a good hand or bluffing. Using this ability, he won the first three games. The other players became suspicious when he won three hands in a row. They suspected that he was cheating. Ranger lost the next two hands on purpose, which alleviated their suspicions. Saying he was tired of losing, he went to a higher stakes table. This time, he won only as often as he lost. However, he always won more money than he lost. After several hours, he had acquired a substantial amount of money. His last stop was the highest stakes table. Again, he won as often as he lost, but even when he lost, it was not as much money as when he won. Each time Ranger left a table, he took a portion of his winnings and hid it in his boot. By the time he reached the highest stakes table, he had enough money in his boot to pay for their room and board, as well as the needed supplies to replace those lost in the Grass People raid. Unfortunately, his winning did draw attention. By the time he arrived at the highest stakes table, there was a small crowd following him. Attention like this was not good. He went to the table with one purpose in mind, to lose.

At the table were three wealthy merchants and one very slick card shark. The merchants wore suits made of the finest wool. They were drinking whiskey and smoking cigars. The card shark wore a silk vest, embroidered with intricate patterns, with a gold watch chain. He had taken off his jacket, exposing the white shirtsleeves with garters around each upper arm. Ranger knew he could beat the card shark. But in doing so, he would draw too much attention to himself. The first few hands were won by other players. Then came a hand with quite a bit of money on the table. Ranger saw his chance. If he won this hand but lost the next to the card shark, all eyes would be on the winner instead of him. Ranger did win that hand. Now they were down to the final hand. The winner would take all. Ranger dealt the cards. Unfortunately, he dealt himself a very good hand, a straight flush, jack of hearts high. Studying the others, Ranger surmised he held the winning hand. If he won this hand, he would not only take all the money, but also establish a reputation as the best card player in Golden Plains City. So, he discarded his middle card, drawing a two of spades. His hand was now worthless. Throwing down his cards, he rose and left the table. The card shark won! He received all the money and all the attention. Ranger slipped out without being noticed, or so he thought.

Upon returning to the Inn, he found the company sound asleep in their rooms. As was his nature, he climbed into bed with his clothes on.

While Ranger was out gambling, Jack was having a private word with the Innkeeper. He asked him what he knew about the Great Rift Depression.

"Best to stay out of it," the Innkeeper said. "There is a well-traveled road that circles just north of the Depression. It takes a fortnight longer, but is much safer. In addition, there are many travelers on that road, in the event you need help." The Innkeeper had just given Jack two reasons for NOT taking the safer road.

"Why," asked Jack, "should we avoid the Depression?"

"There are fell beasts, unnatural creatures, in there. And worse than the beasts, evil lives there," warned the Innkeeper, his voice trembling.

"Have you ever been in the Great Rift Depression?" queried Jack. "NOT on your life!" he emphatically replied.

"I thought those were just old tales. Not to be believed," said Jack, wanting to hear more about the Great Rift Depression.

"Not old tales. I had a guest with half his face torn off. He said some fell creature attacked him in the night. Evil drives them to hate and lust for blood."

"What kind of evil?" asked Jack. "Pandemic evil?"

"Not pandemic, but evil. This evil was older. It was in the Great Rift Depression long before the pandemic came to our eastern shores. They say only the Sharur of Garwalda can vanquish it."

"What is that?" asked Jack.

"It is a mace imbued with a special power that evil cannot defeat."

"Where can I find this Sharur of Garwalda?" inquired Jack. "You can't. I don't even know if it really exits. It might just be an old tale." With that, the Innkeeper returned to his duties.

Jack kept all this to himself. He did not want to upset the others. However, he knew it was destiny that had brought them to the Golden Plains City, and destiny that would take them into the Great Rift Depression.

In the morning, after a filling breakfast, they went to the dry goods store for provisions. They bought new packs, clothing, food, and warm coats. Winston was not happy. He would have to bear the weight of all those provisions.

Winston remembered back to the time he had taken Ponakwa to a dry goods store. He remembered not allowing her to mount him until she bought a warm coat. They were going to cross the snowy mountains, and she would not have survived without a proper coat.

He wondered what dangers the Circle would encounter.

James Black

Chapter 11

Talgor

As the Circle left the Golden Plains City, two unusual things happened.

First, a mountain chickadee circled the company several times. Raven saw it first. "Look," she said, pointing to the sky, "there is a chickadee circling us." The troupe looked up to see it had a black cap of feathers on its head and neck, with white cheek stripes. The wings were dark gray. The body was light gray. The chickadee had a very pointy beak.

"I wonder why it is circling us?" mused Glamdor.

They watched as it circled one more time, then landed on Winston's head. Winston gave a low soft grunt. The chickadee chirped a greeting song. Raven and Winston were the only ones who understood. Then it began to sing a long series of "beeeee, beeeee, deeeee, deeeee, deeeee" sounds. The first beeeee's were high notes. The deeeee's were low. This was followed by a mixture of faster beeeee's and deeeee's, where some of the deeeee's were high, and some of the beeeee's were low, in what seemed like random order.

"What is it saying?" queried Glamdor.

"He is telling us his name and why he has come," responded Raven.

You may recall that J's (Glamdor's) family have very long names. Calvin, his father, has the royal name Rovan Tovan, Tim-Tam-Povan, Maxfield, Okendale, Splitrail, and Sam. Calvin's ancestral name is James-son-son-son. He is the son of James-son-son, who was the son of James-son, who was the son of James. It was impossible to keep track of all those names. That is why he was just called Calvin.

The chickadee had a very long name too. It is too long to recite here. Fortunately for us, he goes by "Beak". "He told us where he was from and why he has come," explained Raven.

"I am from high up in the Silver Mountains, hundreds of leagues east of here. My family has resided there for generations," Beak chirped. Then he launched into his family genealogy. Raven, who was interpreting, spared the company the long list of his family names.

"I was sent by the Unicorn to guide you down through the Great Rift Depression and up the Silver Mountains to the Unicorn's enchanted valley," translated Raven.

The Circle was taken aback. Speaking of the Unicorn was nothing unusual to Beak. He had lived in the Unicorn's valley all his life. But to the Circle, it was a very different matter. This was the first contact they would have with the Unicorn. They suspected the road ahead would be difficult and dangerous. Otherwise, the Unicorn would not have sent Beak to help.

The second unusual thing actually started before the Circle left the Golden Plains City. Ranger, who had been around many men the night before, began to feel lethargic. At first, he thought nothing of it. After all, he had been up late, gambling, which would account for his lack of sleep and tiredness. But as the day wore on, he began to feel worse. By the time Beak arrived, he felt unenergetic, needing to rest.

"Are you all right?" asked Rae. "Just tired from last night's gambling," replied Ranger. However, the tone of his voice indicated more than just being tired.

"Let me look at you," said Alvar. Looking into Ranger's eyes, he saw sadness and depression.

"It's the pandemic," chirped Beak. "I have seen it in many humans on my way here. It is especially bad in the Great Rift Depression."

Raven and J hurried over to Ranger's side. Raven tenderly held his hand. "You are going to be all right," J said, reassuringly.

"I am not so sure," replied Ranger. "The pandemic seems to have a strong grip on me."

Beak chirped, "We need to get Ranger to the Unicorn as soon as possible."

J and Raven's Beauty and Grace were inspiring to Ranger. Their caring words and attention helped him feel better. But it would take the power in the Unicorn's horn to cure him.

"We must go now, no time to waste," chirped Beak.

Ranger mounted his pony. Being on horseback always made him happy. He loved to ride, feeling the saddle beneath him, and the pony's power. Off they went, the last leg of their journey through the Golden Plains.

Beak chirped that the road between the Golden Plains City and the Great Rift Depression was an easy ride, as well as relatively safe.

Alvar was in the lead, with J riding next to him. The Circle put Ranger in the middle, with Raven riding beside him, then Jack and Rae. As always, Winston brought up the rear. He liked that position. He saw himself as the rear guard. His grunts and brays would alert the Circle of any danger coming from behind.

"I have asked Raven about herself," Glamdor confided to Alvar, "but she has always been elusive."

"Raven's heritage is not well known," Alvar replied. "It has been kept hidden because of her father. He has great power. People want to use him for their own gain."

"What power does he have?" asked J.

"J, his name is Talgor, which means Dragon Slayer. Talgor was born in the northernmost kingdom of Norseland, the youngest of six children. His birth name was John. People called him 'John the Fearless.' As a proud young boy, he was daring, afraid of nothing. He would ride wild horses for fun. Climbed dangerous peaks for a thrill. Even fought boys much older than himself, often getting beat up badly."

Alvar continued,

"Like your father, he was born of royalty. And, like your father, when he became of age, he went through the ritual of Nach-Ny-Don-Qua, the ritual that transforms a boy into a man."

"Will I become a man going through Nach-Ny-Don-Qua?" asked J.

"We shall see, we shall see," repeated Alvar. Although, he knew J was already well on his way to becoming a man. The sword, Glamring, and his new name, Glamdor, were the beginning of his Nach-Ny-Don-Qua. Unlike others, J's ritual would take months, not three days.

He continued,

"Talgor began his journey by traveling to Mount Ghor. No one ever went there because of Glaspar, the dragon."

Glaspar's lair was deep inside the mountain. He had been sleeping for years with his hoard of jewels and gold. Talgor climbed Mount Ghor and found Glaspar's cave. Being fearless, he picked up a rock and threw it into the cave. As he did, he yelled, "Anyone in there?" At first, he heard nothing. Then there was a low rumbling coming from deep within the cave. Talgor boldly strode into the cave, calling out,

"Come out, come out, whoever you are."

This irritated Glaspar, who roared, "Who dares disturb my sleep?"

"I did," answered Talgor, proudly.

"Who are you, and who do you think you are to disturb my sleep?" demanded Glaspar.

"It is I, John the Fearless. I am here on my quest of Nach-Ny-Don-Qua to become a man."

John proceeded farther into the cave, following what appeared to be a dim light. He went through a low passage which opened into a giant room. It was filled with diamonds, rubies, sapphires and all sorts of other precious gems. Gold doubloons and silver ingots were everywhere. John's eyes filled with wonderment as he saw the humongous fortune. At first, he did not see Glaspar. Dragons sleep under their treasures just as we sleep under blankets. Glaspar began to stir. Gold, silver, and other jewels fell off his body as he rose up. Drawing himself up to his full height, which was the equivalent of a two-story house, he looked down on John. Then he roared,

"How dare you disturb my slumber. For that, you shall DIE! "

Most people would have run away in mortal fear of the dragon. Not John. He stood his ground. Looking up at the dragon he said, defiantly,

'You can't kill me!"

"And why is that?" retorted Glaspar.

"Because you have not answered the riddle."

"What riddle is that?" demanded the dragon.

"The riddle I am about to give you."

Dragons have two weaknesses. They cannot resist trying to solve a riddle. The second weakness is in their armor. Dragons have scales, not skin. Their scales are thick and tough as diamonds. Nothing can penetrate them. But every dragon has one scale with a small chink, small enough for a knife or arrow to penetrate. The chink is hard to see. You must get very close to see it. John knew this.

John stepped closer to Glaspar. Speaking softly, he recited the riddle. His words were so soft, the dragon had to move closer to hear them. Here is the riddle:

It sleeps in the day and sleeps in the night,

It is very big and not afraid to fight,

Gold and silver, bright and red,

One swift thrust, and it is dead!

As Glaspar started to answer, John thrust his knife deep into the dragon's chink. With a loud wail, Glaspar collapsed to his death. John had slayed the dragon, and thereby inherited all its wealth.

This happened on the very first day of John's Nach-Ny-Don-Qua. The ritual takes three days and nights. Talgor was not only fearless, he was also shrewd. He saw no reason to go traipsing around the countryside after he had slayed the mighty Glaspar. So, he remained in the dragon's cave. While there, he decided on his new name, 'Talgor the Dragon Slayer'. He also began searching through the jewels for the most precious one of all. On the last day, he found it, the Raven Stone. This is a black star sapphire. It is not the largest sapphire in the Middle World. What makes it special is that, in addition to having seven legs, not six, it gives healing powers. The Raven Stone gives its bearer power to heal people.

On the third day, Talgor returned home, without fanfare. His father and the other elders were interested in hearing about his adventures, not expecting to hear anything exceptional. When he told them of vanquishing Glaspar, they did not believe him. It was not until he took the Raven Stone from his pocket, and displayed it, that they believed him.

Alvar said to J, "There are many more tales about Talgor. The only additional thing you need to know at this time is, that Raven is Talgor's daughter. Her name comes from the stone she wears around her neck."

"Raven wears the Raven Stone?" exclaimed J.

"Yes," replied Alvar.

James Black

Chapter 12

Saving a Family

Over the next fortnight, the Circle of Six traveled over 100 leagues down the East-West road. Beak flew ahead, keeping an eye out for trouble, while Winston brought up the rear. They encountered very few travelers. Most were headed west, hoping to avoid the pandemic. A sizable extended family consisting of a brother, two sisters, their husbands and wife, as well as 7 children, were traveling west in three wagons. All the adults were infected with the pandemic, as well as three of the children. Beak, seeing the approaching family, returned to the Circle. He told them of the approaching family and recommended the troupe help.

"All the adults are infected," warned Beak. "If you don't help, they will not make it to the Golden Plains City. And, even if they do, they will spread the pandemic throughout the city."

The Circle discussed the pros and cons of Beak's recommendation and decided to help. Glamdor and Raven rode ahead, Raven clutching her Raven Stone.

"Hello," he said, "can we help you?"

"Well ...," the brother pondered Glamdor's question. "I .... guess you can."

The brother wondered how these young people could possibly help. His next thought was, what are they doing here alone? He wanted to ask them, but at that moment, the older sister cried out in pain and doubled over.

Raven jumped off her pony and ran to the older sister's wagon. She climbed up, wrapped her arms around the sister, and whispered, "You will be better soon." The sister looked up into Raven's face and smiled for the first time.

Beauty and Grace.

It was Beauty and Grace that healed the sister. Her recovery was slow. It took several days. But she did recover.

The rest of the Circle arrived as Glamdor and Raven were ministering to the family. Whispering words of Beauty and Grace to each family member, they began the healing. As with the sister, it was a slow recovery. In the meantime, Rae and Jack started a fire and cooked a hearty dinner. The warmth of the fire, a fine meal, and the encouraging words of Raven and Glamdor, lifted the family's spirits. There were even a few smiles. One of the little girls took Raven's hand. She looked up at Raven and said, "You are beautiful." Raven smiled. "And so are YOU," she replied. "What is it that makes you so special?" the girl asked. "Beauty and Grace," Raven answered.

"What is Beauty and Grace?" asked the girl.

Raven replied with only two words, "This moment."

The girl thought about Raven's reply. She thought about her sick family. She began to realize what Raven meant. Raven and Glamdor had stopped their journey to help her family. They did not have to do that. Helping was an act out of Grace. Beauty was within Raven. Her kindness, sweet smile, and willingness to help a sick family, were part of her Beauty. Self-confidence was another aspect of her beauty.

That conversation permeated deeply into the girl's being. She would remember Raven's two words for the rest of her life. They became her guiding light. The kindness Raven showed her, that day on the East-West road, would become a huge influence on her life. Years later, the girl would turn out to be a great healer.

The family and the Circle slept well that night. The following morning, they shared breakfast, then went their separate ways. As they were packing up, Jack asked the brother if they had traveled through the Great Rift Valley. "No. We took the circle route north around the Valley. We were warned of fell creatures, so we stayed away."

Jack wished the Circle had the time to take the northern route around the Valley. However, it would have added time they did not have.

It took two more days for the Circle to arrive at the East-West, North-South fork, just as the sun was highest in the sky. They ate lunch in silence. Every member of the Circle wished they could take the North-South fork and avoid the danger that could be awaiting them. Without speaking a word, they continued east, dreading what might happen.

Ranger was feeling worse. Glamdor and Raven tried to bolster his spirits, but he was not his old self. She clutched the Raven Stone around her neck.

"If you feel any worse, I have something that will help you," voicing concern for Ranger.

She had kept the Raven Stone a secret from the others. Due to its great value, she did not want to cause the Circle to worry about keeping it safe. But if Ranger got significantly worse, she would let him wear it. Its healing power would hold off the pandemic until they could get to the Valley of the Unicorn. Raven did not know that both Glamdor and Alvar knew she had the Raven Stone. Alvar had instructed Glamdor not to tell anyone she possessed the powerful stone.

The remainder of the day passed without incident. Towards sundown, Beak flew ahead to find a suitable campsite. He found a stream not far from the East-West road with a lush field of grass for the animals. Raven started a fire while Rae and Jack prepared dinner. They had bought a side of cured pork from the butcher, next door to the dry goods store. They drank fresh cold water from the stream and warmed-up pork ribs. Following dinner, the troupe settled in for a good night's sleep. Beak and Winston guarded the camp.

Early the next morning, Beak woke the Circle with his "rise and shine" song. The high note *beeeee's* and low note *deeeee's* that Beak squawked were quite irritating to human ears. The company rose right away.

"We must be going now," chirped Beak. Birds are much faster than humans because they can fly. J thought about how much faster he could get there if he flew. Since the others could not fly, it would not do him much good. He ate a light breakfast, as did all the others, of oatmeal and water. They did not bother with a fire.

By late afternoon, the Circle had covered the last section of the Great Golden Plains. The sun was beginning to cast long shadows. Looking east, J could see the Silver Mountains. The sun's rays made the snow-covered peaks shine brightly. Between him and the mountain peak, he saw only a dark shadow.

"Why is there only darkness between us and the Silver Mountains?" J asked Jack, who was also gazing at the Silver Mountains.

"The darkness you see is the Great Rift Valley." Jack's words were unsettling.

"Is it true, what they say about the valley? That fell creatures lurk there?"

"Yes, it is true. I have seen them myself," answered Ranger, who had feebly walked up behind J and Jack. "Have you seen them, Jack?" asked Ranger.

"No." replied Jack. "I have never been in the Great Rift Valley. I always avoided it by using the circle routes. The Rift was, and still is, too dangerous. But now, we have no choice."

Chapter 13

The Hammer

Who WAS this man?

His birth name was Pavelli, which means purify. He was born in the kingdom of Di-Wal-Nach, located in the southeast corner of the Middle World. The kingdom is a dazzling, sun swept land. The inhabitants have beautiful golden tan (sometimes brown) skin, black hair, and brown eyes. While they can speak the common language of the Middle World, their native tongue is Di-Wal-Nachish.

His parents loved him very much and wanted him to live a happy and meaningful life. They thought the priesthood would provide that. On his eighteenth birthday, his father took him aside and said:

Pavelli my son, you are the pride of my life, the apple of my eye. Your mama and I are very proud of you. We love you with all our hearts. This is a sad time for us, but a beginning for you. As you know, when a Di-Wal-Nach boy reaches the age of eighteen, he must leave his family, in search of his destiny. That time has come.

Your mother and I have always felt the priesthood would be best for you. Being a priest, you could minister to the sick and poor. Helping your fellow Di-Wal-Nachians is a noble calling. We have watched you grow into a caring man. We saw how you helped rescue and protect others. Do you remember the time your little sister fell into the great Di-Wal-Nach River? Do you remember how you jumped in and pulled her out before she drowned? And there was the time we were visiting my brother who lived on the edge of the Misty Jungle. You jumped in front of the hungry tiger, waving your arms wildly and yelling, keeping it away from your young cousin. You placed her safety above yours.

These are the reasons we feel your destiny is to become a priest. Your mother and I want to help you, so we have enrolled you in the Seminary of Sacred Devotion.

Pavelli was not sure he wanted to be a priest. His natural inclination was to use the sword instead of the word, but he did not want to disappoint his parents. So, off to the Seminary he went.

Upon his arrival, Pavelli was interviewed for the purpose of finding a suitable priest to guide and educate him. Pavelli displayed exceptional intelligence and was eager to learn. Unfortunately, he did not excel in the "obedience" department. The priesthood required three commitments: a vow of poverty, celibacy, and obedience. The last commitment would prove to be a problem.

Brother Obedient was the priest given charge of Pavelli's training. Pavelli tried, with all his might, to learn obedience from his priest. Alas, he simply could not change his nature. After several months of dedicated effort, Brother Obedient went to the Abbot. "Father," he said, "I am not the right teacher for Pavelli. Try as I may, he still is unable to be obedient. Can you please help?"

The Abbot, who oversaw the seminary, knew of Pavelli's nature. He had anticipated that Brother Obedient would eventually ask for his advice. The Abbot counseled him,

"I think the Wandering Priest would be the best teacher and guide for Pavelli."

The Wandering Priest no longer resided in the Seminary. He traveled the countryside, ministering to the needy. Pavelli flourished under his tutelage. Traveling exposed Pavelli to many different peoples, ideas, and cultures. They started their journey in Di-Wal-Nach, heading north. When they came to the frontier, Pavelli asked the Wandering Priest, "What is beyond the border?" The priest said, "Let us discover that together." Their travels took them to the northern kingdom, where Talgor was born. They even went to Zarlaka too. For three years, they traveled and ministered together. By the time they returned, Pavelli had become a man. He had learned the ways and customs of other cultures. Along the way, he studied the martial arts, learned to cook, and read ancient manuscripts whenever he could find them. As his study progressed, he acquired knowledge of the Great Queen, Matakwa, and the prophecy of the boy and girl. This prophecy, in particular, fascinated him. Pavelli knew, somehow, he would help fulfill it.

When they finally returned to the Seminary of Sacred Devotion, he was given the Test of Priesthood. Seven priests, over a five-day period, questioned Pavelli to determine his suitability for the priesthood. He failed the test miserably, demonstrating little ability to obey. Pavelli was sent home, shamed and humiliated that he could not join the priesthood. His parents were disappointed. While they wanted him to be a priest, it was more important, for them, that he find his true calling. And, so, once again he set out to find his destiny.

Pavelli traveled for five more years. As with the Wandering Priest, he again visited many kingdoms. He traveled around and finally through the Great Rift Depression. He climbed high up in the Silver Mountains. Far above the Unicorn's Valley. Even in summer, it was cold and snowy that high up in the mountains. Late one particularly cold afternoon, he spied a small log cabin. Smoke was coming from the chimney, which meant the occupant was either inside or nearby. As he approached, he saw an old man chopping firewood.

"Hello," Pavelli said, "would you like some help chopping?"

The old man looked at Pavelli, nodded, and handed him the axe. With a mighty blow, Pavelli swung the axe down on a very thick piece of wood, splitting it in two.

"Your strength and ability are amazing," said the old man. Pavelli said nothing, as he continued splitting the next piece. "You must have lots of experience splitting wood," the old man continued. Again, Pavelli did not respond. He continued splitting the wood and did not stop until all of it was split.

"Come in and have something to eat with me," invited the old man, "you must be hungry after splitting all that wood."

"Thank you," replied Pavelli. The aroma of simmering stew greeted him, inside the cabin. Pavelli hadn't realized how hungry he was. The stew's aroma made his mouth water. They sat at an old wooden table made of log planks. Chairs were log stumps. The old man lived a simple life. Nothing inside the cabin was decorative. Everything was functional. Even the cupboard consisted of a series of horizontal log planks nailed to the log wall.

"Tell me," asked the old man, "what are you doing way up here?"

'Seeking my destiny," he replied.

"I see. Have you found it?"

"Not yet," answered Pavelli.

"Well," continued the old man, "perhaps I can help. First, we must fill your tummy."

He continued refilling Pavelli's bowl until he was finally full. When he was satisfied that Pavelli's hunger was satiated, the old man reached over and opened the drawer in a small table. Taking out a parchment roll, he said, "Read this."

Pavelli unrolled it and began reading. Here is what it said:

Sharur of Di-Wal-Nach, the legend.

A young boy, who lived in Di-Wal-Nach, was gazing out his bedroom window, when he saw a shooting star. It came close to his house, landing with a thud in his backyard. The boy, curious to see what had landed, climbed out his window. He did not want his parents to know he was still awake. What he saw was a glimmering golden-color stone. It appeared to be just a little larger than his fist and felt warm to the touch. He snuck back through his window with the stone and climbed into his bed, deciding to keep the stone a secret from his parents. He was afraid he would be in trouble for sneaking out at night. A few days later, he did show the stone to his Ma and Da, saying he had found it on his way home from school. They thought it was nice, but nothing special. "Look," said the boy, "it has a golden glow and is warm to the touch." Neither of his parents saw the golden glow nor felt its warmth. "Take it to the healer, see what he says," said the boy's Ma, who was concerned that the boy might be imagining the stone had features it did not really have.

The healer did not see the glow or feel the warmth either. But he had heard the local wizard tell stories of such a stone.

"I will send him (the wizard) a message," he told the boy.

The very next day, the Wizard arrived. Looking at the stone, he muttered something to himself and then said, "This stone must be kept safe. It has great power and must not fall in the wrong hands." The boy, not wanting to get in trouble, gave it to the Wizard.

"The stone is here. Would you like to see it?" asked the old man. Pavelli was not aware, at that time, that the old man was, in fact, a wizard. And, he had been the keeper of the stone for many years. It had passed down through many wizard's hands to his. His choice to live high in the Silver Mountains was to keep the stone away from evil people.

"I would," replied Pavelli. The old man reached into the drawer and pulled out the stone. Its golden glow surprised Pavelli. "Here," offered the wizard, "hold it." The stone was warm to Pavelli's touch. "Does it feel warm to you and glow?" "Yes," answered Pavelli. "I see and feel nothing," stated the old Wizard, shaking his head.

"The stone is called Garwalda, which means *'servant of the sacred'*. Read on," he instructed Pavelli.

It is foretold that Garwalda will become the head of a sharur. Forged high in the Silver Mountains, its name will be Sharur of Garwalda. Only he who forges the sharur can wield its magical powers. He who wields the Sharur of Garwalda will be called THE HAMMER. His destiny is bound to the Sharur. Together, they will protect the Middle World.

"Am I that young man? Is this then my destiny?" asked Pavelli.

"You are. You are THE HAMMER," the old Wizard replied:

I will teach you how to forge the Sharur. It shall have a golden handle and Garwalda at the head. If you throw the Sharur, it will go as far as you wish it to. It will obey your every command and use its power according to your will. And, it will always return to your hand. Because it has great power, you must be very careful to only use it for good.

Over the next few weeks, The Wizard taught Pavelli, The Hammer, how to use the forge. It took only half a fortnight for Pavelli to master it. Once accomplished, he began forging the Sharur. Many sacred oaths and incantations were spoken by the Wizard. When it was completed, the old man told The Hammer, "Seek your destiny. Find the Circle. Protect them from the horde of fell creatures. Help them to eradicate evil." Pavelli was not sure exactly what that meant. Nevertheless, he began his quest.

Over the next two years, The Hammer prepared to fulfill his destiny. He sought to discover and understand the habitat of fell beasts. It did not take him long to learn that the beasts roamed in the Great Rift Valley. Armed with the Sharur of Garwalda, he descended into the Valley. Searching, he found their lairs. He found all the paths leading through the Valley. He stayed until his knowledge of the Great Rift Valley was unrivaled.

The Hammer also found two forms of evil. There was the pandemic, which infected only people. The second was much older and darker. It was in the form of Fell Beasts. Fortunately, the darker form could not exist outside the Great Rift Valley.

Finding the "Circle" was the biggest task. The Hammer, as he was referred to by then, did not know what the old Wizard meant by "Circle". He sent spies out to watch and listen. One of his spies, in the gambling house of the Golden Plains City, saw Ranger gambling. The spy suspected Ranger might have something to do with the Circle. He followed Ranger back to the Inn. He waited until the company had gone upstairs to sleep, then asked the Innkeeper if he had heard the company mention the word "Circle". In fact, the Innkeeper had. He waited until the following day to see which way the company rode. As soon as he saw them riding east, the spy was sure he had found the Circle. Word was sent to The Hammer that the Circle had left the Golden Plains City, headed for the Great Rift Valley.

The Hammer lurked in the Great Rift Valley, keeping his presence unknown to all. He saw a bird known to reside in the Valley of the Unicorn (Beak) and suspected the Circle must be nearby. At one point, he even faintly heard voices. Although he could not make out their words, he recognized one of the accents. It was the same as the Wizard from the Silver Mountains.

The Hammer settled down for a nap just before the horde of fell beasts attacked the Circle. Hearing the melee, he rushed to the scene, forgetting to bring the Sharur of Garwalda with him. He leapt into the middle of the Circle. His destiny was to save them.

Chapter 14

Hills and Valleys

"YOU SAVED US!!!" cried Rae. Joy and jubilation ran through the Circle, quickly followed by the shocking realization of what had just transpired. The entire troupe had been moments away from death. A man from out of nowhere had saved them. The forest was still burning. Dead creatures were burning, giving off a putrid smell. Smoke was hanging in the air, too thick for Beak to find a way out. Moreover, the trail was covered with fallen trees and burning vines.

No one spoke, letting the feelings of almost dying, then being saved, sink in. Jack was the first to break the silence.

"Who are you?" he asked the man.

"I am called The Hammer."

"How did you know to save us? How did you know we were here?" Jack inquired. The Hammer smiled, then answered,

"Destiny."

Another moment of silence, as the Circle tried to grasp what had just happened, and to comprehend what "destiny" meant.

"We must leave this place right now," said The Hammer. "The fell beasts will gather in greater numbers and return to finish what the others started."

"How many are there?" asked Rae. "More than you can count. I will guide you to the eastern bank of the Valley. There you will be safe." The Hammer whispered something to the Sharur. Then he raised his arm and released it. The Sharur flew east, passing close to the ground, magically clearing the trail.

The company gathered themselves up, mounted the ponies, and followed The Hammer. Even though he was on foot, he could easily run as fast as a horse could trot. Raven wondered how fast The Hammer could really run, but hoped she would not need to find out. If that happened, it would mean there were too many fell beasts even for The Hammer to fight. It took three hours to reach the eastern side of the forest. As before, the climb to the rim was steep. The Circle had to dismount and walk their ponies. Beak was the only one to ride. After the "Battle of the Fell Beasts", as it was later to be called, Beak was too shaken to be of any help. He remained perched on Winston's head until they reached the top of the rim and had traveled another two leagues. Even then, Beak was worried the beasts might come after them. The Hammer stopped to survey their surroundings. The land was a continuation of the Golden Plains. Tall grass growing on rich fertile soil. A mild breeze flowed over the tall grasses, making them bend in undulating waves. It was eerily tranquil. Raven found it hard to understand how evil could be lurking only a few leagues away. Gazing west, she could see only the Golden Plains. The Great Rift Valley was just a dark line in an otherwise sea of golden grains.

"Would you like to camp here for the night?" asked The Hammer. None of the company spoke. They did not need to. The Hammer could see the fear etched on their faces. They were still too close for comfort to the Great Rift Valley. "There are still a few hours of daylight," The Hammer said, in a reassuring voice. "We can push on. I know a campsite near the Misty River. We can reach it by nightfall if we keep up a swift pace." Again, no one spoke. They resumed their positions behind The Hammer and off they went. Beak was glad to be riding on Winston's head. Winston appreciated his company, too. They spoke of green pastures for Winston and berry bushes for Beak.

When they arrived at the campsite, the Circle was feeling better. They were still a little worried, but trusted that The Hammer would keep them safe. Jack and Rae built a fire, while Glamdor and Raven prepared the food. As they were working, Alvar quietly consulted with The Hammer. Their spirits lifted during dinner. Food has a way of making people feel better. They even kidded around with each other.

J teased Raven about attacking a fell beast with her little knife, how inadequate it was. He really wanted to communicate how brave he thought she was. Unfortunately, it backfired. Instead of feeling brave, Raven was overwhelmed with emotions. Fear returned. Tears streamed down her face. She began to tremble. Rae reached out to hold her. She too, felt fear. Tears also began to stream down *her* face. The whole company fell silent as they relived their own feelings.

Ranger broke the silence. "It is good that we are all alive," he said in a hushed voice, "and mostly well." The others agreed and began to speak their truth about what had happened. They expressed how afraid they had been. They complimented each other on their bravery. They all were grateful to The Hammer for saving their lives. Even Alvar, who rarely complimented anyone, thanked The Hammer.

As the fire burned down to embers, sleep came to the Circle. They laid out their bedrolls and fell into a deep sleep. It was the first night in several days they had slept soundly.

The next morning, Jack and Rae restarted the fire. This time, Ranger and Alvar set out the food. As they were eating, J asked The Hammer,

"Will you continue with us to the Unicorn's Valley?"

"No," replied The Hammer. "I must return to Di-Wal-Nach, my home. The pandemic has taken root there. There are disturbing reports of strife among my people. They need me and the Sharur of Garwalda to slow its progress. YOU," he said in a loud and urgent voice, "must get to the Unicorn. Only THEN will you have the power to drive the pandemic from our shores, never to return."

"Well then," urgently spoke Alvar, "we must not tarry. Gather up your things. We must make haste. Beak, are you ready to lead us to the Unicorn?"

Beak, who had regained his strength, chirped, "Follow me!" He fluttered his wings, flew up above the troupe, and urged them to hurry.

The Hammer traveled east with the company until it intersected with the Norseland-Di-Wal-Nach road, which ran north and south.

"Will we see you again?" asked Raven. "You will." He did not say anything more. Left unspoken were the words, "Once again I will come to your rescue."

The Circle waved goodbye to The Hammer. He waved back, turned, and faster than a horse could gallop, ran not south, but north. The Circle was confused, as his home was in the south. They did not know he had one very special proposal to make before he returned to his home in the south. They were sad to see him leave. But comforted to know he would return.

Ascending up the Silver Mountains was arduous, but not dangerous. The East-West road followed valley floors. On each side of the valleys, tall snowcapped peaks rose high into the sky. "Only five more leagues," chirped Beak, "then we take the North Valley road. The road runs north for two days."

"Two more days," thought J. How well he remembered Ranger saying it was only a two-day journey through the Great Rift Depression. "Are there any dangerous animals, fell beasts, on the Unicorn Valley road?" asked J. "There are no fell beasts. Only natural animals. Most are harmless or afraid of humans. The only danger comes from grizzly bears. As long as we keep a safe distance, and they are not hungry, they pose no threat."

What Beak told them was true. The road did run north for two days. What he neglected to tell the Circle was that the road turned into a foot path for a league, then nothing. No road, no path, no trail. Yet, it was another five days to the Unicorn Valley. There was nothing but wilderness between the end of the road and the Valley. Without a guide, travelers would likely become hopelessly lost. Many would perish for lack of food or from inclement weather. Mountain storms often brought several inches of snow, even in the summer. One party that was caught in such a storm, became hopelessly lost. They were without food for days. Some even tried to eat their leather shoes. Fortunately for the Circle, Beak knew the way and would guide them to the Valley. Even so, they would have to climb steep forested hills, descend into ravines, even cross three raging rivers.

At the intersection of the East-West road and the North Valley road, they stopped to rest. J felt saddened to depart from the East-West road. He had traveled it for fortnights. Leaving it was, in some respects, like leaving a friend. Their rest was brief. Riding north, Glamdor turned back and whispered "Goodbye," to the road. He wondered if he would ever travel that road again. It seemed to him that leaving the road was like leaving his old life. He was transforming, becoming Glamdor. He was sad to leave his old life behind. On the other hand, he was committed to see what lay ahead of him.

The next two days passed without incident. By now, the Circle had become seasoned travelers. They were able to ride many leagues without stopping. When they did stop, it was to rest the animals. Beak was in great spirits. Each day brought him closer to home. He did some scouting, but most of the time, he rode on Winston's head.

At the close of the second day, they came to the end of the North Valley road. "What happened to the road?" asked Jack. Beak flew up into a tree limb. He wanted distance between him and the Circle when he told them what lay ahead, fearing they might do him harm. He chirped away, and Raven translated. The company was disappointed by the news. However, by then, they had been through so much, that something like this did not surprise them.

"Are you sure you know the way?" Jack asked, apprehensively. "I do," chirped Beak confidently. "You will recall that I flew all the way to the Golden Plains to find you. I grew up in these mountains. I *can* find my way home. Follow me," he chirped, then fluttered his wings and flew north.

For the next several hours, the Circle followed Beak and the trail through the dense forest. The trail turned gradually into a footpath, and finally came to an end. Beak was waiting for them there, perched on a log. "Straight ahead is a rise. The other side is quite steep. There is an old game trail you can follow. However, it is too narrow and steep to ride. You will have to walk your ponies. Once we get to the bottom of the valley, we will cross the first of three rivers."

The footing was difficult, like Beak had warned. Nevertheless, the Circle made it to the top of the rise and down the other side. The river, on the other hand, proved to be quite challenging. It was about one hundred feet wide, strewn with boulders. Water rushed over and around them, causing many rapids and much turbulence.

"Follow me," chirped Beak, "there is a crossing not far from here." For a bird that can fly, "not far" is very different than it is to humans and animals who walk. The riverbank was steep and very hard to navigate without falling in. What took Beak only a few minutes to fly took the Circle over two hours. They were exhausted when they finally arrived at the crossing. They stopped to rest and eat a light meal. Crossing the river was without incident. Up another steep ridge and down the other side they went. By the time they reached the second river, the sun had set. Beak said he would keep watch so the Circle could sleep, which they did, soundly. Crossing the second river was more difficult. Like the first, there were boulders and rapids. Beak knew about an easier crossing, "not far away". Knowing how long "not far away" meant in travel time, they decided to cross right where they were.

Surprisingly, Ranger's condition had greatly improved. As the distance between the Circle and the Great Rift Valley grew, so did his strength. "I will cross first," he said. "Give me a rope. Once across, I will tie it to a tree. The rope will give you support in crossing the river." Carefully, Ranger made his way to the other side. Only once did he slip and fall in. Although he was swept downstream several yards, he was able to regain his footing and continue on to the other side. He tied the rope around a stout fir tree directly across from the company. "It's ok now," he yelled, "come on over." One by one, the troupe crossed, bringing with them their ponies. Winston proved to be difficult. He did not want to wade into what he considered a raging torrent. Ranger crossed back to the other side, bribed him with a carrot and lured him into the water, all the way to the other side. Their clothes were soaking wet, but they all had made it across the river. This time, Glamdor and Raven built the fire. The company took off most of their clothing and hung them by the fire to dry. They decided to camp by the river for the night.

The next few days were some of the most difficult ones of the entire journey. It was tough climbing up and down one steep ridge after another. The only saving grace was that they did not have to cross a river, at least. There were streams, some wide, but could be crossed without fear of drowning.

As the sun rose over the mountain tops, casting long shadows in the valleys below, Beak chirped happily, "This is our last day. By nightfall, we should be in the Unicorn's Valley!" Under normal circumstances, the Circle would have been very happy to hear this news. But they were too exhausted, at that point, to feel celebratory. Their only focus was to push on to the end. Beak did not tell them there was one more river to cross. They knew it was ahead, and did not need to be reminded.

Without speaking to each other, the troupe ate, loaded up the ponies, and continued riding east. Up yet another mountain. It was not as steep as the previous ones, but proved to be more treacherous. So many fallen logs to step over, and many holes in which the ponies could step and break a leg. At the top, they rested.

"Do you see the next mountain?" Beak chirped. "On the other side of it is the Valley of the Unicorn."

J and Raven gave a sigh of relief, which turned out to be premature.

"Look down there!" exclaimed Jack.

They looked down to see a raging river. The last and biggest river, which they had to cross. It was too wide and deep to cross on foot. They figured they would have to build a raft. After descending to the Valley floor, the Circle began piecing together a raft. They used fir trees that had been blown over during a windstorm. They fashioned a large pole which would steer the raft away from boulders. The raft could support only three people at a time. Alvar, J and Rae went first. Before leaving, Ranger fastened a rope to a giant fir tree. The other end he tied to the raft. After crossing the river, the remaining travelers could use the rope to pull the raft back to their side.

After successfully crossing the river, the Circle climbed the last steep slope. At the very top, they laid eyes on the Unicorn Valley, at long last.

James Black

They had arrived!

Chapter 15

The Valley of the Unicorn

The view was magnificent. Having encountered so many difficult obstacles, the Circle appreciated its beauty all the more. Their eyes gazed upon the lush, green valley. Grass for the ponies, fields of grains and corn for the humans. Small villages with plentiful gardens dotted the countryside. The life-giving river flowed through the middle of the Valley, bringing water to fields, gardens, and villages. They saw a small city situated at the foothills of the east end. There, a temple had been built to honor and worship the Unicorn. On its top was a giant statue of the mythical creature. The entire Valley was ringed with high mountains. They had taken the only way in. The mountain peaks provided protection from the outside world, especially evil. The Circle were the first "outsiders" to enter in three generations, although they did not find that out until later. After descending into the Valley, they came to a village.

The village was similar in structure and layout to the villages they had passed through before on their journey. There was a village square, through which the main road passed. Flanking its sides were small streets lined with thatched roof houses. They did not notice the existence of any Inns. "Probably," thought Rae, "there is one in the city, which is not too far away." The villagers were very different from the ones the Circle had encountered so far. They smiled. They were friendly. There was a warmth and happiness that permeated the village. Before, upon entering a village, they had been met with distrustful stares. Now, they were greeted with warm smiles. They stopped at the square to water their ponies and Winston. Beak, who had been proudly riding on his head, chirped a greeting to the villagers who had come out to see their visitors.

"You are the Chosen Ones," said an old woman, steadying herself with a cane. "I have waited all my life to see you. To be honest, I was afraid you might not come in time for these old eyes to gaze on the saviors of the Middle World." Her smile was infectious. Everyone in the Circle could feel her warmth. It seemed to radiate from her. Other villagers arrived. They too had the same kind of warmth as the old woman. J and the other members of the Circle began to realize that they were in the presence of Beauty and Grace.

Since leaving Alvar's cave, the only Beauty and Grace they had experienced was their own. Before the Circle was formed, Beauty and Grace were rare to be found. Here, it was commonplace. "Go to the City of the Unicorn," said the old woman. "Your reception has been prepared. A great feast awaits."

"How did you know we were coming?" asked J. "That and all your other questions will be answered in time, but first, you must go to the city. A grand reception is awaiting your presence. I will take you. All the villagers are there, anxiously looking forward to greet you."

Winston nuzzled up to the old woman. "You must be the mule so often mentioned in the sacred scrolls." Winston raised and lowered his head in agreement. By the time they had arrived at the Valley, most of their provisions were gone. Winston's load was light. With help from Ranger, the old woman was lifted up onto Winston's back. "Follow me," she said, and nudged Winston forward. And so, they did. The Circle, led by Winston and the old woman, passed through the Valley, crossing over the river on a sturdy wooden bridge. The bridge was a great relief to the Circle, being that they didn't have to swim.

The procession entered the city, greeted by cheering people lining the main street. The old woman was smiling from ear to ear. Her position of honor, at the head of the procession, was the crowning moment of her life. They rode to the temple gate. Monks dressed in bright yellow robes greeted them, helped them off their ponies, and escorted the Circle into the great banquet hall. Winston and the ponies were led to a lush field where they could graze to their heart's content. The Circle expected to be greeted by the abbot of the monks. Instead, a committee of monks welcomed them.

"Welcome to the City of the Unicorn," they chanted in unison. Some chanted in high notes, others low, creating a dissonant sound. The monks were singing in different keys, not trying to harmonize with the others. J thought this was strange. He made a mental note to ask about it later. After the welcoming chant, each member of the Circle was escorted to a separate room to bathe. Male and female attendants were there, as appropriate, to help. J unbuckled Glamring, setting it down on a small stool. Then he removed his clothing. "I will have these cleaned for you," said the attending monk. He picked up the clothes with one hand and reached for Glamring with the other. The hilt glowed red with heat when the monk touched it. "Ouch!!" he cried out, dropping the sword. He did not know that once Glamring came into the possession of the Chosen One, no one else could touch it. "Are you alright?" asked J. "My hand burns. I must put it in cold water," he replied, wincing with pain. The monk hurried out of the room.

J enjoyed his bath. He remembered bathing with his brothers, how they would play and splash water all over, until Naomi came in and made them behave. He missed his brothers, and his Ma and his Da. He was far away from them, no longer the boy in the bath. J was entering into manhood.

Rae and Raven soaked for a long time in their baths. Each tub had salts and oils with the scent of lavender. Their bodies relaxed in warm pleasure. After soaking for quite a while, they began to scrub their bodies. Jack, Ranger, even Alvar vigorously scrubbed. It was not just dirt they were trying to wash off. It was the evil that resided in the Great Rift Valley. Evil that had permeated their clothes, their hair, and even their skin. They scrubbed until they were almost raw. Finally, they felt clean.

Each was given robes according to his/her stature. Only Alvar refused, preferring his own robe. Jack and Ranger were given bright red tunics and dark brown breeches which had a gold stripe running down the outside of each leg. The tunics were adorned with golden buttons and a silken sash. Both Rae and Raven were given cream-colored, high-waisted, long, flowing gowns. The sleeves were fringed with white lace and pearls. Each was wearing pearl earrings which matched their pearl necklaces. J wore the uniform of an imperial soldier. Like Ranger and Jack, he had a red tunic and brown breeches. In addition, on his shoulders were golden epaulettes and around his waist was a thick leather belt with a golden scabbard to hold Glamring. He cut a very handsome figure, indeed.

The feast was held in the great banquet hall. The room was large enough to hold most of the inhabitants of the Valley. Great platters of roast beef, baked potatoes, fresh corn on the cob, greens of all types, and apple cider were served. Jack noticed there was no wine. He quietly asked one of the monks serving him why. "Oh," the monk replied, "wine is good for the soul. It can take away sadness, even pain. Here, we have something much better."

"What is that?" asked Jack quizzically.

"Beauty and Grace," replied the monk.

It was true. That was what made this Valley different. That was what made the villagers smile when the Circle had entered. "Who needs wine, when we have Beauty and Grace?" thought Jack. With that thought in mind, he looked over at Rae and winked. She smiled, lowered her head, then slowly lifted it up, looked into his eyes and blew him a kiss.

The feast lasted for several hours. Between courses, the guests danced and shared stories. Jack made a point of dancing with Rae, even if the dances did not involve partners. After the last serving of dessert, an old monk told the story of Kolakie (pronounced Koo laaaa key) and the Bear:

Once upon a time, there was a young girl named Kolakie. She lived deep in the woods in a log cabin with her mother and father and five brothers and sisters. It had been a long cold winter with lots of snow. Spring was late, but finally arrived. Only a little snow remained in the hills. Daffodils were in bloom. Kolakie loved to see the bright yellow flower shaped like a trumpet on its green stem. She picked a few, then skipped down the path leading to the stream. When she saw how fresh and inviting the water was, she slipped off her shoes and waded in. Standing in the middle of the stream, she heard a stern voice ask,

"Who are you and what are you doing in MY stream?"

She turned to see a mother bear and three cubs standing where she had just taken off her shoes. "I am Kolakie," she replied, meekly. "I did not know it was YOUR stream. Please forgive me. I did not mean any harm." Mother Bear growled.

"Mother Bear," Kolakie entreated, "just think of me as one of your cubs. One who likes to wiggle her toes in the stream and pick daffodils." The Mother Bear growled again. But this time, the cubs ran into the stream to play with Kolakie and wiggle their paws in the water. The three cubs and Kolakie splashed and played in the stream, while their mother watched protectively.

At first, it was just a speck in the sky. Then it grew larger. As Mother Bear watched, she saw its shape form. It was a giant hawk! The hawk was watching the cubs and Kolakie, with hungry eyes. It folded in its wings and dove straight at them. The hawk had not noticed the Mother Bear. As it raced towards its prey, she jumped up and ran into the stream, screaming, "Run, run for your lives, come to me!" They all did, including Kolakie, who would have made a nice gourmet meal for the hawk. They huddled under the Mother Bear as the hawk's talons, poised to grab, narrowly missed Kolakie. With a mighty roar and swat of her massive paw, the Mother Bear struck the hawk, killing him.

"You saved me!" cried Kolakie, holding tightly onto Mama Bear's leg. She looked down at Kolakie, "I did, and from now on, you are one of my cubs," Mama said. From that day forward, Kolakie was a member of the bear family. Over several years, the cubs and Kolakie grew into adults and started their own families. Kolakie's children played with the cubs' children. Every spring, when the daffodils bloomed, Kolakie would pick a bunch and take them to Mama Bear.

So, when spring comes, and the daffodils bloom, you should pick a bunch and take them to YOUR mother, and thank her for being your mother, just as Kolakie did for Mama Bear.

After the monk finished, all of the guests went to their rooms, and slept soundly, basking in the beauty of his story.

Chapter 16

The Unicorn

The Circle rested for three days. They ate fine food, indulged in many warm baths, even played the monks' favorite ballgame. The object of the game was to identify which monk ended up with the ball. J played first. There were six monks and one ball. One of the monks held up the ball for J to see, then he tossed it to another monk. That monk tossed it to a third monk, who in turn tossed it to another monk. The ball was tossed back and forth among all six monks, faster and faster. J tried to follow the ball with his eyes, but he could not keep up with it. Making matters worse, all had shaved heads and were dressed in identical crimson robes. Finally, the monks stood in a line with their hands behind their backs. J had to guess which monk had the ball. He chose the wrong one. Feeling disappointed, but not wanting to give up, J played again. His second attempt was better. He chose the monk next to the one with the ball. J's final attempt was not even close. Rae was next to play. Like J, she had no luck. Jack was determined to win, at least once. Alas, the monks were still too fast for him. He could not keep up with the ball.

Raven eagerly implored, "Let ME try!"

The game began. The ball passed so quickly from one monk to another, it was impossible to follow its path. The monks formed into a line, hands behind their back. Big smiles on their faces. What the Circle did not know was that NO ONE had ever won the game. Raven wrapped her hand around the Raven Stone, which was on a leather string around her neck. She walked over to the monk on one end of the line. Looking into his eyes, she smiled. The stone felt cool to her touch. She approached the second monk in line, and gazed into his eyes. The stone remained cool. She continued down the line. When she stood in front of the fourth monk, the stone became warm. Raven did not identify the monk. Instead, she continued down the line. After looking into the eyes of the last monk, she stepped back and gave a sigh, letting go of the Raven Stone. The monks smiled, feeling confident she had not identified the monk with the stone. Raven turned, facing the Circle, her back to the monks.

"This is very difficult," she confessed. Then, she whirled around and pointed to the fourth monk.

"YOU!" she exclaimed.

The monks were shocked! No one had ever won before!

"How did you know?" asked the monk on the end.

"Girl Power!" asserted Raven, proudly.

The monks, as one would expect, were all male. "Girl Power" was a new concept to them. From that day on, girls were held in special esteem at the monastery.

The Circle and the six monks retired to the dining hall for lunch. It was a jovial affair, with happy stories and silly jokes, such as, do you know how to tell a monk from a pumpkin? Ask a monk. He will go into a long, detailed, and boring description of the obvious differences between a pumpkin and a monk. The pumpkin will considerately spare you the pain of listening by saying nothing.

J asked, "When we first arrived, the chorus of monks all sang in separate keys, not in harmony. Why?"

For a moment, sadness appeared on the monks' faces, followed by silence. J was afraid he had said something that upset them. He felt their sadness. The monk sitting across the table noticed J's sadness and said to him,

Long ago, the monks had an abbot, whose name was Jarwall. Abbot Jarwall wanted to create a great temple to honor and worship the Unicorn. All the people living in the Valley, including the monks, worked to build it. The work was hard but rewarding. The abbot worked day and night, planning, organizing, directing, even working side by side with the laborers.

As the temple neared completion, Abbot Jarwall's demeanor changed. He stopped working with the laborers, declaring, "A man of my importance should not stoop to physical labor." After the temple was completed, he ordered a special hymn be written for the dedication ceremony. The hymn was harmoniously ethereal, praising the Unicorn. At the last moment, just as the ceremony was to begin, Jarwall had the hymn changed from praising the Unicorn to praising himself!

The monks were shocked! They revolted! Abbot Jarwall was cast out. "Never again," declared the monks, "shall we have a leader."

"That is why we don't have an abbot," said the monk to J. "We never sing in harmony to remind us of our human frailties. Power corrupts. Absolute power corrupts, absolutely."

After lunch, the Circle was ushered out onto the veranda, where a dozen chairs were arranged in a circle. "It is time," said one of the monks, "to prepare you."

"Prepare us for what?" asked J, inquisitively.

"To meet the Unicorn," he replied.

There was a long silence.

"Your journey here," continued the monk, was necessary in order to prepare you." J and Raven were confused.

"You could have flown on Alvar's griffin, or J could have flown himself."

"I figured we'd better hide from evil, which was why we went on foot," J said, with more of a question in his voice than a statement.

"That is true. Evil would have known your location if you had flown. However, you would have been here before evil could react, perhaps. Moreover, evil already knew you were coming to this valley. The reason for your journey was to prepare you. Neither you, J, nor you, Raven, were ready to accept the power of the Unicorn. The power magnifies and enhances the qualities of its bearer. If the bearer is not properly prepared, the power will enhance the wrong attributes."

"J," the monk continued, "do you remember what Alvar told you when you first wanted to learn how to use a sword?

"I do," replied J, who thought back to the three steps Alvar had taught him.

"What did Alvar tell you?" asked the monk.

"He said, first I needed to learn about Beauty and Grace. Next, I was to learn how to NOT need to use a sword. Finally, he would teach me swordsmanship," answered J.

"Good," said the monk. "Have you learned about Beauty and Grace yet? Have you learned how NOT to use the sword?"

"I think I have," replied J, and added,

"The Innkeeper's daughter, Naomi, was healed from the pandemic by Raven's Beauty and Grace. In that village, I learned how it would save the Middle World. I went into Timmon's camp, a gang of highwaymen, without a sword. Only using words, I was able to change the whole gang for the better. Finally, with Glamring's flaming power, I smote fell beasts. Now I see WHY our journey was necessary. Now, I believe, Raven and I are ready to meet the Unicorn."

"The time has come," said the monk, to meet the Unicorn!"

There was a moment of silence as the Circle pondered what the monk had just pronounced. For many fortnights, the Circle had been on a long and dangerous journey to meet the Unicorn. Finally, that journey was coming to an end. For a moment, they felt relief that the journey was over. In the next moment, they realized that the next journey and a new chapter in their lives was about to take on a drastically new direction.

Raven, not wanting to think about what kind of challenges the next journey might present, put her mind to a different question. One that had bothered her since first encountering the monks.

"What is your name?" she asked the monk.

"We don't have names," he replied. "We are servants of Beauty and Grace. Our birth names were cast aside when we took the vow of "Eternal Commitment to Beauty and Grace". We wish only to be seen as their devotees."

Raven continued, "Well, you are human, aren't you? Therefore, each one of you must have some unique characteristics."

"We do," he agreed. "Each of us has a number. It can be used when it is necessary to identify one of our order."

"I see," Raven continued. "What is YOUR number?"

"12, 421."

"How can anyone possibly remember a number like that? There must be over one hundred monks here. That makes for lots of numbers," Raven said. She shook her head in bewilderment and thought to herself, "They need a woman in this place to straighten out this NUMBER problem!"

"The moon will be full tonight," said 12,421. "The Unicorn will appear at its zenith. Rest now. Dinner will be brought to your rooms. You will want to prepare yourselves for his arrival."

The troupe retired to their quarters. It was not long before everyone ended up in Alvar's room. They were too anxious to wait alone. At first, they made small talk, such as, how comical Winston looked with Beak riding on his head. Then, the conversation turned serious. J asked Alvar,

"What will happen tonight?"

"That remains to be seen," he replied. "Jack and I have extensively studied the ancient scrolls. We have been able to piece together some of what has already happened, and what WILL happen. Most of what we know has already transpired. We know that the Circle of Six would travel to the Unicorn. We know that two of the Circle, a boy and girl, are the Chosen Ones. We know the Chosen Ones will receive the Great Queen's power from the Unicorn. And finally, we know the Chosen Ones will drive evil out of the Middle World, never to return. That is all we know."

"What happens to the Circle after tonight?" asked Raven.

"We don't know," replied Alvar. "We shall have to wait and see."

More silence followed, as each member of the Circle contemplated the future and what their role in it would be.

As the moon was rising to its zenith, 12,421 came to fetch them. "It is time," he said. "I will take you to the meeting place."

Monks had lined the path to the "Shining Knoll", where the Circle would meet the Unicorn. No one spoke, not a monk or a member of the Circle. Each was lost in his or her own thoughts. The knoll was ringed with monks. Only the Circle waited at the top. Ranger saw the Unicorn first.

"Look!" he exclaimed, pointing to the north. They all looked in astonishment. There was the Unicorn, as it had been described in the scrolls. His mane and tail gleamed silver in the moonlight. His horn was a rainbow of colors, radiating bright and beautiful. His wings were both powerful and graceful. His body was magnificent with powerful legs and a long gloriously arched neck. He flew straight to the knoll, landing with elegance and grace. J and Raven looked at each other, then at Alvar. Alvar nodded for them to approach the Unicorn. Holding hands, Raven and J did so. Looking at each other again reassuringly, confirming they were in this together, each reached out with their free hand and wrapped it around the horn.

At first, nothing happened. Then, slowly, joy began to fill their minds and spirits. They felt as if a great weight had been lifted from their shoulders. They felt as if they were flying. In fact, they were. They had risen with the Unicorn, far up into the sky. Looking down, they saw the Silver Mountains and the Unicorn Valley. They could see from Kambuka to the eastern shore, from Norseland to Di-Wal-Nach. Visions of people they had encountered on their journey appeared. They saw the family they had saved on the East-West road. The children were happy, their parents were content. Naomi, the Innkeeper's daughter, was singing her lullaby about the beautiful girl. Even Timmon had changed his ways for the better. J and Raven realized how their own Beauty and Grace had made the Middle World a better place already.

The next vision was disturbing. J and Raven saw distress throughout the east. From the Silver Mountains to the eastern shore, villages, towns, even great cities were suffering from the pandemic. Evil had permeated the people. Joy had been driven away, replaced with negativity and mistrust. Families were filled with strife. Old friendships had been replaced by loneliness. Crops were failing. Food shortages were prevalent. Raven and J understood what lay ahead of them. They envisioned the daunting task of bringing Beauty and Grace to a world infected with evil. But now, the power of the Great Queen resided in them. The power to drive out evil. A task that would not be easy, that could even cost them their lives. Yet, it must be done. It was their destiny

Chapter 17

Broken Circle

The return of the Chosen Ones to the "Shining Knoll", riding the Unicorn, marked the beginning of a new era. They were no longer that same boy and girl who had traveled as part of the Circle. They had been transformed by the power of the Great Queen. They were now mature beyond their years, appearing strong and confident. A soft light glowed around them, radiating Beauty and Grace. The other members of the Circle were speechless, even Alvar. All stared in awe and admiration.

The Unicorn, whose horn was now dim, having given the Great Queen's power to the Chosen Ones, leapt up into the sky and flew directly towards the moon.

"What happened?" asked Jack. "You seem like different people."

"We saw Beauty and Grace," asserted Raven. "We looked into the future. We saw what must be done."

"Did you see OUR future?" Jack asked, excitedly. "Tell me, what is MY future?"

"That is something you must discover on your own," Raven advised him, with wisdom beyond her years … wisdom bequeathed to her by the Great Queen. She continued,

"It is time to break up the Circle. Jack, you will travel to the north. Find Talgor. Tell him to locate and tame the Rainbow Dragon. Together, you, Talgor, his brother Ian, and the Dragon will drive evil from the land. The north will then be free from the pandemic. Songs will be sung of your great deeds by many generations to come.

Rae, henceforth, you are to be the bearer of the Raven Stone. Travel south to Di-Wal-Nach. Seek out The Hammer. Together, you will eradicate the pandemic there. Songs will be forever sung of your great deeds, also."

Jack and Rae glanced at each other, feeling unanticipated loss, knowing they were to be separated. Raven continued,

"When the pandemic is driven from the Middle World, you, Rae, and you, Jack, will be joined in marriage. I have foreseen you wed on an enchanted island."

Jack and Rae were still sad at the thought of their parting, but were comforted knowing their hearts would always be joined, and one day they would be united in marriage.

"Ranger, you already know your path," Raven added. "You will travel east with Glamdor and me. Together, we will drive evil from its stronghold in the

Eastern Kingdom. Once it is gone, you will take your rightful place as King. As for you, dear Alvar, your path was not revealed to us. It remains a mystery."

No one spoke as the Circle left the knoll. It would be the last time all six would travel together. Feeling the future loss of their traveling companions, each member's heart was filled with sadness.

As the Circle returned to the temple, the sun's rays broke over the eastern ridges of the Silver Mountains. Even though it was a beautiful morning, none of the company could appreciate it. Breakfast had been prepared, which they ate with very few words. Having been awake all night, they retired to their rooms for a nap. It was late morning when they arose. After a light lunch, they prepared their traveling packs and met at the portico of the temple to bid their final farewells. Jack hugged each of the company goodbye, as did Rae. They turned to each other. Jack was crying. Tears streamed down Rae's face as they embraced each other. They kissed, a tender kiss of love and devotion. With that, they mounted their ponies. Jack rode north, Rae, south. Everyone wondered how long and what would happen before they would be all together again.

The remaining four mounted their ponies. Winston, who would continue with them, brayed noisily. Beak flew overhead, chirping his goodbye song. They rode east, leaving the enchanted Valley of the Unicorn behind.

The Circle was broken.

Chapter 18

Good and Evil

"Life is a struggle between good and evil," Alvar sagely observed. "The journey ahead will certainly engage us in that struggle. Evil awaits us! Time is of the essence. Our destiny is to eradicate the pandemic. Are you ready for the fight?"

Glamdor placed his hand on the hilt of his magic sword, Glamring. "I am!" He was well aware of the danger they would face, having defended the company against the fell beasts in the Great Rift Valley.

Raven was ready too. Her father, Talgor, was known as the dragon slayer. He was fearless. She desperately wanted to emulate him and be fearless, too.

Ranger's destiny would take him in a different direction. He would be fighting along with the Chosen Ones to eradicate evil. But his true destiny was to take his rightful place as King of the East. He would rule from the Silver Mountains to the Eastern Shore. His kingdom would border on the north with Norseland, and on the south with Di-Wal-Nach.

Jack and Rae were destined to marry.

"The problem with destiny," continued Alvar,

is evil."

Just when you think you understand your destiny, evil may intervene. Jack is destined to marry Rae. The question is, will he survive long enough to marry her? And, even if he does, they may, or may not, live happily ever after. Will the eradication of the pandemic result in the death of Jack or perhaps some of the others, Glamdor, Raven, Rae?

The struggle between good and evil is the only destiny we can be certain of.

Chapter 19

North, South, East

Beak's cousin, Squeak, guided Jack northward. Although the terrain was as rugged as it had been coming from the west, there were no rivers to ford. Traveling alone, Jack's horse was able to maintain a faster pace. He did miss the Circle, and much to his surprise, Winston's complaints. His braying from behind had been reassuring to Jack. Now, there was only silence. It took only a day and a half to reach a narrow road, which would take him to the Norseland-Di-Wal-Nach road.

Squeak chirped, "Follow this road west. In half a day, you will arrive at the Norseland-Di-Wal-Nach road. From there, travel north."

Jack thanked Squeak and watched as the bird fluttered south, starting the trip back to his home in the Valley of the Unicorn.

Rae's travels south were more difficult. She was guided by Squeak's sister, who chirped incessantly. She chirped on about her family, friends, likes and dislikes, even her favorite food, which was flaxseed. Rae's pony had a difficult time keeping up with the bird. Partly because the terrain was rough, but also because she was sick of the incessant chatter and kept reining the pony in. At the end of the second day on their journey south, they came to a wide river. It was too deep to wade across and too deep and wide to swim across. Sitting down on the riverbank, she tried to figure out how to cross. Squeak's sister was of no help. She kept chirping, "All you need to do is fly across."

Rae thought to herself, "What a stupid bird, ... doesn't she know that women and ponies cannot fly?"

She considered building a raft. Regrettably, she did not have an axe to cut down trees. There might be a better place to cross, but she realized if there were, the chirping sister probably would have guided her there. Rae built a fire to warm herself in the frigid air and ate a meal of porridge and drank hot tea. Thankfully, the river nearby provided plenty of water.

"Fly across," the bird kept chirping. After the sun had set and the moon rose, Rae looked up to the sky and thought to herself, "How can I possibly FLY across the river?" Then she realized that she was holding the answer in her hand! Raven had given her the Raven Stone. Its power was what she needed. In her loudest voice, she called out,

"Unicorn, Unicorn, PLEASE HELP!"

Shortly, his form appeared in the moonlit sky. She watched in wonderment as he landed right in front of her. Grabbing her pack, abandoning her pony, she mounted the Unicorn. The pony was glad to be abandoned. He returned to the Valley of the Unicorn where he spent his remaining days grazing on lush rich grass and basking in Beauty and Grace. For him, the journey was thankfully over.

The Unicorn flew southwest. It took only a few minutes to arrive one furlong east of the Norseland-Di-Wal-Nach road. Rae spied the road as they approached. Slipping off the graceful creature and making her way to the road, she wondered if Jack was also on that same road. They could then both be on the road but traveling in opposite directions. Rae felt the road was her connection to Jack.

Meanwhile, the remaining four, Raven, Glamdor, Ranger, and Alvar rode east. They did not have a guide ... one was not needed. A secret trail existed which led east, ultimately intersecting with the East-West road. After circling the Great Rift Valley, the East-West road continued east, which the remaining four of the Circle followed. Twenty-two leagues east of where the Circle departed from the road, it turned northeast for thirty-five leagues. Then it turned east again, leading straight to the eastern shore. The secret trail intersected the East-West road in the middle of the northeast diagonal. This meant that the four remaining travelers would have to travel about thirty-five leagues before intersecting with the East-West road.

The first afternoon was somewhat difficult. After leaving the city, they climbed to the rim of the Unicorn Valley. Raven and Glamdor took one last look before heading east. The image of the Valley was imprinted forever in their minds. During difficult times, they would recall that image and the Unicorn, which would strengthen their resolve. They followed the trail down the other side of the rim into a dense forest. Night fell early in the dark forest. None, however, wanted to stop. Urgency was upon them. Especially for Glamdor and Raven, who had foreseen how quickly the pandemic could spread. Alvar held up his staff, the tip giving off a soft glow, just enough to see the trail. They continued on for several more hours. At was almost four in the morning when Winston refused to take another step. Try as they might, he would not budge. So, they settled down for a nap. Three hours later, after Winston had been bribed with grain, they were off again, moving silently through the forest. Occasionally, they heard animal sounds. Most were small, like raccoons and chipmunks. They came across a mother bear and three cubs, playing in a stream. Deciding not to disturb or upset the mother bear, they made a wide berth around the bear family.

"I wonder if that was the same bear family Kolakie met?" Glamdor whispered, trying not to disturb the animals. "Can't be," replied Raven. "That story took place long ago. As I recall, Kolakie's children and the cubs' children played together."

"You are right, AS USUAL," Glamdor agreed.

Late in the afternoon, a mountain storm blew in. The wind howled great gusts swayed the treetops. Weak limbs broke off. One almost hit Ranger in the head. Thinking it was too dangerous to continue, they took shelter under a giant oak tree. As soon as the wind passed, they mounted their ponies and resumed their journey east. They rode through that night and the following day, resting only at Winston's insistence. They maintained their pace the next day and night, arriving at the East-West road mid-day on the fifth day. The first village on the East-West road was only a three-hour ride away. They arrived about four in the afternoon.

They were shocked to see the extent of the pandemic. Shops were closed and boarded up. The main street was strewn with litter. Weeds were growing everywhere.

"We must meet this challenge head-on," Glamdor proclaimed. They rode into the village square. Glamdor was on the lookout for the village leader. His office was located just on the east end of the square. Several guards were stationed out front. They were slovenly dressed, unshaven, with unkempt uniforms and scraggly hair.

"I wish to speak to the Burgermeister!" Glamdor's voice was authoritative.

"He's busy!" a surly guard replied.

"We must see him, now!" insisted Glamdor. The party dismounted. The guards reached for their swords. Glamdor's hand rested on the hilt of Glamring. It was not a time to use swords. Words would be more effective. Raven, in her feminine way, walked up to the surly guard and said,

"Please, sir. It is a matter of great importance." As she spoke, her right hand reached up to the guard and gently stroked his cheek. He fell under the spell of Beauty and Grace.

"He's in there," the guard said, pointing to the front door.

The four entered, walked down the once ornate, but now derelict hallway, and entered the Burgermeister's office. It was full of empty bottles. Paper strewn everywhere. He was drunk!

"Get out!" he screamed. "I am not seeing anyone today. Guards!" he yelled. They came running in.

"Why did you let them in?!" he screeched. "Throw them out!"

It was time for the sword! The guards drew theirs. Glamdor, smiling, not in the least afraid, drew Glamring.

"Are you sure you want to throw us out?" said Glamdor.

The guards looked at the flaming sword, lowered theirs, and quickly backed out, leaving the Burgermeister to fend for himself.

Alvar spoke, "The last time I visited here, your town was prosperous. Now it looks quite different. Was it the pandemic?"

"Get out! You are not welcome here!!" screamed the Burgermeister.

Once again, using her feminine Beauty and Grace, Raven said, "Dear Sir, you are a man of great importance. Please grant us a moment of your time. We wish only to bring happiness to you and your village."

"I doubt you can do that," he replied, but with much less hostility.

"Please allow us to try," Raven pleaded. "It will cost only a few moments of your time."

"Well, I guess that can't hurt," his words losing all their hostility.

Raven took the Burgermeister's hand, walked him to his couch and sat beside him. Glamdor, who had returned his sword to its sheath, sat on his other side.

"Can you tell me what happened?" Raven's kind and caring voice disarmed the Burgermeister.

"It all happened so fast. Our village was happy and prosperous. Without warning, the pandemic ravaged us. It came with a traveler from the east. He said he had come to help us with the fall harvest. But he spread the plague instead. We lost all desire to harvest our crops. Disagreements broke out over property boundaries. Time was wasted, and eventually, fights broke out everywhere. I was unable to stop them. There were just too many of them. When winter came, we did not have enough food. Stealing, looting, even forming a gang to force villagers into giving them their food.

The following spring was a little better. With warmer weather, villagers could go outside. They were no longer forced to be cooped up together. We did plant some crops and started to tend a few gardens. But then, just when we thought the worst was over, a hailstorm blew in from the Silver Mountains and ruined our crops. We lost hope, as you can see."

Raven put her arm around the Burgermeister. At first, he shed a few tears. They were quickly followed by a flood of sobbing tears. His pain was very real. Both Glamdor and Raven felt it.

"We will help you rid the pandemic from your village." Glamdor's words were tender and compassionate. The Burgermeister's heart opened, feeling Raven's and Glamdor's Beauty and Grace.

"You are the town leader," said J. "You can lead the villagers back to happiness. Call them to the square for a village meeting."

The Burgermeister made the arrangements for a village meeting the following day. In the meantime, Glamdor and Raven spent more time talking with him. He told them that his wife and son had died from the pandemic. His farm was in ruins and he felt he had no reason to go on living. He found escape in alcohol. They sat with him, listening with empathy to his tragic story, then told him he had a very big reason for living. He was the head of the village. All of the villagers were dependent on him for leadership. He needed to give them hope.

"Without hope," Glamdor explained, "all is lost. People need hope. They need to feel their lives are important. You can bring that to them. Show them they need to care for each other. Tell them that the crops they harvest, the fruit of their gardens, and the children they raise are important. Speak to their hearts."

The Burgermiester did not realize that Raven and Glamdor were speaking to HIS heart. His mind did not grasp their words, but his heart did. He began to smile. He saw how important his life was to the villagers. How he could be instrumental in driving out the pandemic.

He saw a glimmer of Beauty and Grace.

"What is Beauty and Grace?" he asked.

Raven gently answered,

"Beauty is your unique talents, gifts, and abilities. For you, it is your natural ability to be a leader. Grace is the way you use your talents to make the Middle World a better place. Tomorrow, when you hold the village meeting, let your Beauty shine."

Tears again filled the Burgermeister's eyes. "Yes," he said. "I see, I see what you are saying. I understand."

"We need to prepare for tomorrow!" said the Burgermeister, with hope and happiness in his voice, for the first time.

He called for his guards. "Tomorrow, there will be a village meeting. We need to clean up everywhere and prepare." He split the guards in half. One group was sent out to notify the villagers of the meeting. The other half worked with him to clean up the town hall and the town square.

"I think our work here is almost done," Glamdor said, feeling the urgency now of getting to the next village. "What do you think, Raven?" She was not sure. "Perhaps one of us should stay to help with the meeting tomorrow."

"I can stay," volunteered Alvar. "I know the Burgermeister, having visited him before. As his friend, I can support him in the event evil tries to thwart his efforts to bring hope to the village.

Beauty and Grace

Early the next morning, Ranger, Raven, and Glamdor rode east, leaving Beauty and Grace behind.

James Black

Chapter 20

Rae Meets the Girl

While Ranger, Glamdor, and Raven were riding east (Alvar remained to help the Burgermeister), Rae was walking south on the Norseland-Di-Wal-Nach road. The road passed through a forest of tall evergreen trees. The trees were like giant spires, rising far up into the sky. Their lowest branches started over a fifty feet up. Some of the oldest trees were baby saplings during the reign of the Great Queen. They had weathered storms, forest fires, floods, even droughts. Rae stopped to gaze up. As she did, she heard a faint cry, coming from the forest. It was the sound of a young girl. Rae called out,

"Hello. Anyone there?"

She heard another faint cry, then, "Over here."

Rae followed the sound and found a young girl, maybe thirteen or fourteen, huddled up against the trunk of a giant fir tree. She was wearing only a light muslin dress and no shoes. Her hair was knotted and scraggly, her face unwashed, and she was shivering.

"Are you hurt?" Rae asked, very concerned for her well-being.

"No," meekly replied the girl.

"Here, let me help you," Rae said, as she took off her coat and wrapped it around the shivering child. Then, she took her in her arms, trying to provide comfort. After holding her for several minutes, Rae took a loaf of bread from her pack. Offering it to the girl, she asked,

"Can you eat something?"

The girl looked up, nodded, and accepted the bread. Stuffing a large bite in her mouth, she muttered,

"Thank you."

Rae wondered how the girl could have wound up in this forest, without proper clothing. She waited until the girl was warmer and not so famished, to ask,

"How did you come to be here, in this forest?" asked Rae, empathetically. "You don't have to tell me if you would rather not."

"My mother," she began, "married a mean man after my father died. My stepfather would drink too much. When he did, he became angry and abusive. I was afraid of him. I told mother to leave him. She didn't. I told her again, but this time, I said if she did not leave him, I would run away. So, here I am."

"Was it the pandemic that made your stepfather that way?" inquired Rae.

"He was that way before. The pandemic made him worse," she spoke, with tears in her eyes.

"I will take care of you. I am here to stop the virus," Rae reassured her.

They spent the night together under the giant fir tree, wrapped together in Rae's blanket. Rae wondered if the giant tree had seen others spend the night under its branches, and under what circumstances. The following morning, Rae shared her food with the girl, whose name she still did not know, gave her a pair of shoes to wear (two sizes too big), and they made their way back to the road. Frequent travelers called it the "ND" road. Norseland-Di-Wal-Nach had too many syllables to bother with.

They followed the ND road south for most of the day. The girl's home was north of where Rae had found her. Thus, each step took her farther away from pain and suffering. Late in the afternoon, they came to a large village. It was obvious the pandemic had already infected many of the villagers. Many of the houses looked completely neglected. The town square was unkept and overgrown with weeds and vines. There were two Inns, one at each end of the square. Both were in no better condition than the houses. Rae was not sure which Inn they should choose to spend the night. The girl tugged Rae's sleeve. Rae turned to look at her. She whispered,

"It is not safe to stay here. Sometimes, my stepfather drinks with his rowdy friends in these

Inns. I know a place south of town. We can stay there."

Rae nodded in agreement. They hurried away, hoping not to be seen by any of her stepfather's friends. Once safely out of town, the girl pointed to a small hill, saying,

"There is a small stream just over that bank. We can camp there, even make a fire, without being noticed." She started gathering firewood. Rae set out what little food was left. They ate in silence. Rae boiled water over the fire and steeped tea for them. As they were sipping the hot tea, Rae said,

"I am called Rae, what is your name?"

"My name is Said," (sed), replied the girl. "Said is an interesting name," commented Rae. The girl did not reply. Rae continued,

"I am traveling to Di-Wal-Nach in search of a man called The Hammer. Have you heard of him?"

"Oh yes!" said Said. "He is known throughout all the southern kingdoms."

"Would you like to help find him with me?" asked Rae.

"I would," replied a smiling Said.

"We will have to get you proper traveling clothes, and SHOES," replied Rae, whose smile matched Said's.

That night was the first sound sleep Said had had in a long time. She felt refreshed the following morning and was eager to get on the ND road.

"The next village has a dry goods store where we can get clothes, provisions, and even SHOES!" said Said, excitedly.

By midmorning they arrived at the store. Said's eyes were wide with excitement, knowing she was about to get a real pair of shoes. Her stepfather had not allowed her to wear shoes, for fear of her running away. The shopkeeper found a pair of walking shoes that fit her perfectly. Said beamed with delight. Rae also bought her trousers, a shirt, warm overcoat, even a hat. She also bought more provisions for their journey. She bought dry goods to eat, blankets to keep warm, as well as other sundry goods. As Rae was shopping, Said noticed a big jar on the counter full of lollipops. Her mouth watered, her eyes were filled with wonder. As much as she wanted one, she did not mention a word, fearing she would appear greedy. Rae asked the shopkeeper where they could buy ponies. The shopkeeper's brother owned the livery in town and had ponies for sale.

"Good," said Rae to the shopkeeper. "We will return for our belongings once we have ponies to carry them. Oh!" Rae said, remembering something she had forgotten, "do you have lollipops?"

"I do," replied the shopkeeper.

Looking at Said, Rae said, "Well, girl, pick out as many as you want."

Said beamed, jumped up and down with joy, then gave Rae a huge hug. They found the livery and purchased two ponies and a mule. Said asked, "Why a mule and not a pony?" Rae smiled. She considered telling Said about Winston and the Circle but decided to wait until she knew more about the girl. Rae simply added, "Mules are good pack animals." Said asked the livery owner, "What is the mule's name?"

"Jackson," he replied.

Rae broke out in laughter. "A good name!" she exclaimed. "We will call him Jack."

They returned to the dry goods store and loaded up their provisions.

And so, they began their journey south together.

Chapter 21

Grumpelton

Grumpelton was the next town on the East-West road. It was larger than a village, but not big enough to be a city. The name came from its founder, George Grumpelton, a burly man with unbounded energy. His vision was to create something that would make the town unique and well-known. This, in turn, would attract people and further the town's commerce. As he was considering possibilities, he came upon the idea of "cattle". None of the towns or cities on the East-West road were known especially for cattle. George vowed to make Grumpelton the cattle center of the East-West road. He would build the "Cattle Palace", where travelers could marvel at all things "cattle". His first project was to procure pasture lands in which to raise his cattle. The palace would come later, after there were sufficient profits from the cattle, to erect the building. It took four years to complete the project. It was three stories high (very tall in those days) with a giant steer on top. The steer stood thirty feet tall with twenty-foot-long horns. Travelers could see the massive statue from two leagues away.

In his waning years, George created "Eastward Ho", an annual cattle drive. Each fall, cattle were driven down the East-West road all the way to the eastern shore. At each village, town, and city, the drive would stop for cattle to be auctioned off. He always saved his best cattle for the Eastern Capital, where many wealthy people lived. For many decades, long after George Grumpelton passed away, the town flourished, as did Eastward Ho. Unfortunately, Eastward Ho was a "vector" for the pandemic.

Ranger was the first to spot the steer atop the Cattle Palace. It was an amazing sight. "Look," he said, pointing to it, "there is the steer!" The other two looked in awe at the giant statue. Winston was apprehensive. He did not like what that statue symbolized. Cattle were to be eaten. Although he was not a steer, people did eat horse meat, even mules from time to time. He also remembered that Naomi told him she would make him into a pot roast if he did not bring J back safe and sound.

In the magical land of Kambuka, children could fly, and animals could speak. Animals could speak in other kingdoms as well. However, they never did. It wasn't safe. Creatures that had "unnatural" abilities were considered with suspicion and feared. A talking mule could very well be suspected of being possessed by evil. People who are ignorant often resort to violence, out of fear. It would not take much for a few suspicious men to kill a talking mule. Winston had no intention of winding up dead, due to ignorant men.

Winston's apprehension grew stronger as they approached Grumpelton. It turned into fear when Ranger pointed to the steer. They stopped to get a better look at it. When they started towards it, Winston refused to move. He stood with his legs firmly planted. Glamdor dismounted. He tried to coax Winston to walk. The mule refused to budge.

"What is it, Winston?" Glamdor whispered in his ear. "Why won't you budge?"

Winston looked at Glamdor, hoping the Chosen One would figure out why he refused to move. Alas, Glamdor did not. Winston felt he had no choice. In a muffled voice, the mule said,

"There is a trap ahead. Men in the city are waiting to kill you."

"How do you know this?" Glamdor whispered back.

"Mule intuition," replied Winston, dryly.

Glamdor turned to the others and said, "I think there is danger waiting for us in Grumpelton."

Ranger asked, "How do you know that?"

"Mule intuition," answered Glamdor. "That is why Winston refuses to move."

The party discussed several options about what to do. They considered the bold move of riding directly into the city. That was ruled out, because they did not know what awaited them. They talked about sneaking into the town, after dark, to reconnoiter. That, too, was ruled out for fear of being caught. They even considered sending Winston in alone as their spy. Winston brayed a defiant "NO!" Finally, the trio decided to wait for Alvar.

Alvar spent the afternoon helping the Burgermeister with the cleanup. Wizards don't do manual labor. Sweeping, picking up, weeding, these are things Wizards never do. Not helping, however, would certainly not demonstrate Beauty and Grace. So, Alvar decided to do what he did best. Something he had avoided thus far. He whispered a magical incantation to his staff. The stone on its end glowed as he circled it over his head. A breeze suddenly came from the west, blowing down the East-West road into the main square and out the other side of the village. It passed through the village like a giant broom, sweeping the streets, boardwalks, even the village square, clean.

"Can you drive the pandemic out of our village too?" asked the Burgermeister, who was standing next to Alvar, surveying the swept streets.

"Each villager must do that for themselves," he replied in his wizardly wisdom. "As Burgermeister, your task is to show them the way."

"How do I do that?" he asked, very unsure of his ability to show the villagers the way.

"Beauty and Grace," was all Alvar said.

The next day, the villagers who could, assembled in the village square. Some were too infected and sick to come. Some arrived in family groups. There had been arguments between families over pasture boundaries. As the groups assembled, they began to air their complaints. The Burgermeister, standing on the dais watching the melee, became worried. Alvar spoke another incantation to his staff, raising it high above his head. A wave of bright light radiated from it, and swept through the crowd. The villagers fell silent. Some tried to speak, but no sound would come out.

"You have their attention now," said Alvar. "The spell will last only a few minutes. I suggest you say what you need to say, now!"

"Dear fellow villagers," the Burgermeister began, "I am so sorry the pandemic has brought suffering and pain to you. I too have felt its cruel grip. Like many of you, I have lost loved ones. But all is NOT lost. Hope is here. We can defeat this plague! Together, we will drive it out of our beautiful village."

He paused to let those words sink in. Then he continued,

"HOW? you may ask. How can we drive evil out of our village? I will tell you. Yesterday, I was visited by an old friend," he said, reaching over and patting Alvar on the shoulder. "He and his traveling companions showed me the way. I am here today to show YOU. You can defeat the virus within you."

"BEAUTY and GRACE!"

He went on to explain what those words meant. As he did, a few of the mothers began to smile unwittingly, expressing their own Beauty and Grace. Next, the children began to smile. The men were last to smile. By the time the Burgermeister finished his speech, smiles were everywhere. Alvar's spell faded, after which the villagers began speaking civilly to each other.

The assembly slowly dispersed, returning to their homes and farms, feeling that hope had returned. Hope for the future. Hope that life was going to be better. Hope that soon turned to certainty. Within hours, the entire village was certain their future would be bright.

Seeing that "hope" had returned to the village, Alvar knew his work was done. He bade goodbye to the Burgermeister, then rode east to join the others.

He found them camped a league west of Grumpelton. They asked what had happened in the village, wanting to hear good news, before giving Alvar bad news. He described how the Burgermeister's words had moved the villagers. He told of their smiles and how Beauty and Grace started to germinate in each villager's heart. The four travelers ate together. After dinner, they drank tea while Glamdor advised Alvar of what challenges lay ahead.

Alvar had a pensive look on his face. After a few minutes, he whistled to his staff, then raised it, as he had done in the village earlier. The staff echoed the whistle throughout the woods. Suddenly out of nowhere, a flock of ravens swooped down, landing on branches of the trees surrounding the party. Winston looked alarmed. Beak resting on his head was one thing. A whole flock of ravens was another thing. Fortunately, they remained perched on the branches, intending no harm. Alvar invoked a magical chant. It sounded something like this:

Wo wo, na na, do,

Wo wo, na na, go,

Wo wo, na na, see,

Wo wo, return to me,

Wo wo, what did you see,

Wo wo, tell me.

The ravens took off, leaving the branches, flapping their wings as they rose into the sky.

"Now we wait," said Alvar, as he poured another cup of tea.

Throughout the evening and late into the night, the ravens flew in and out of the camp, relaying news about the city. There were three groups of men hiding next to the East-West road. They had swords, knives,

and axes. Within the city, men were stationed on
rooftops as lookouts. They were all facing west. The
saloons were full of men, drinking and cursing. This
did not bode well. Glamdor wondered if this was what
they could expect to confront as they traveled further
east. Had they ridden into Grumpelton, it would have
led to their demise.

"As I see it, we have two options," said Ranger.
"One is to bypass the town entirely by circling around
it, then travel east. The other is to circle around it,
but instead of traveling east, we could enter
Grumpelton from the east, catching them by
surprise, since they are expecting us from the west."

"There is a third option," Raven suggested. "We
could bypass the town, like Ranger said. Then we
could return when the Eastward Ho cattle drive
starts. Many of the men will be on the drive, leaving
the city less guarded."

"When will the drive begin?" asked Glamdor.

No one was quite sure.

"IF we bypass Grumpelton and follow the road
east, we can help other villages. When the cattle drive
passes through them, they can alert us," Raven
offered as a solution. The other travelers agreed that
was the best plan. At four in the morning, well before
the sun was up, the party made a wide circle around
Grumpelton. By the time the sun rose, they were well
out of sight and back on the East-West road.

Chapter 22

Roseville

It was early evening when the party arrived at Roseville, the village just east of Grumpelton. GLAMDOR suggested that they wait cautiously just on the outskirts of Roseville, so he could spend a quiet moment with Winston. The mule was his usual self, complaining about the heavy load he had to bear, but had no sense of imminent danger. They slowly entered the village, looking for any signs of danger and the pandemic. There were many signs of the pandemic, but no signs of danger.

Fear reflected in the eyes of almost every villager they encountered. They rode into the square, where the only Inn was located. Like the first village they encountered, most of the houses were in disrepair. The Inn was also unkempt. Ranger suspected there had not been any guests staying there in quite a while. Dismounting their ponies, and tying them to the hitching post, they entered the Inn.

"Hello! Anyone here?" called Ranger. No reply. Again, he called "Hello. Are you open?" This time, the Innkeeper's wife appeared from a door behind the front desk.

"Yes, what do you want?" her voice quivering with fear. "Lodging for the night and dinner," Ranger said in a kind voice, but too masculine for the frightened woman.

"Please," Raven's voice was gentle and feminine, "we are weary from a long journey. Could we rest here?"

"I guess so," replied the woman, relieved not to have to deal with the men. Raven empathized with her fear, especially of men. "You are kind to take us in," assured Raven, in an understanding tone. The woman's fear lessened a little. "We have only pot roast for dinner," offered the Innkeeper's wife. GLAMDOR chuckled to himself and thought, "Winston's favorite."

After settling into their rooms, they went down for dinner. The dining room was empty. First, the wife brought a pitcher of water, then bread and butter. The pot roast was served in a huge tureen with a large ladle and individual bowls. After they had finished, the Innkeeper's wife came to collect the tureen and bowls.

"Can I help you?" asked Raven. Without waiting for a reply, which Raven anticipated would be "no", she rose, picked up the bowls, and headed for the kitchen. Raven knew the wife would not talk in front of the three men, but might when they were alone. She went to the sink and began washing the bowls.

"You don't have to do that," said the woman. "I don't mind," replied Raven. "Besides, I don't get the chance for girl talk, traveling with three men."

"Sadly, neither do I," said the woman. "Why is that?" asked Raven.

"My husband died from the pandemic. I was left here alone to run the Inn. The only customers who come here are ruffians from Grumpelton. They get drunk and cause trouble. I am afraid of them."

"Isn't there a sheriff or town constable who would help you?" asked Raven. "No, we are too small for that. In the past, we relied on the constable from Grumpelton for help. Alas, he died from the pandemic. Now we have no one to protect us."

"What about the men here in Roseville? Can't they help?"

"Many are too weak, others are afraid."

A plan began to form in Raven's mind. She waited until the Innkeeper's wife had retired for the evening. She told the others about the ruffians. "We can handle a few ruffians," GLAMDOR said, placing his hand on the hilt of Glamring. "We will have to," Raven agreed. "But this an opportunity for us to help the village men rid themselves of the virus." They formulated a plan, which they would start implementing the next morning.

Before the sun was up, GLAMDOR and Ranger had gone to the livery with the ponies and Winston. The livery owner was suspicious of them until Ranger gave him a gold coin. There are times when money can be indispensable.

"I understand that ruffians from Grumpelton come here and cause trouble. Is that true?" asked Ranger.

"Yes," replied the owner.

"We could help you stop them," offered Ranger.

"How?" he asked.

GLAMDOR drew Glamring from its sheath. The man stared in wonderment at the flaming sword. He felt an inkling of "hope" for the first time in a long while.

"Gather a few men, meet us this afternoon at the Inn. We will formulate a plan to deal with these ruffians," Ranger promised.

That afternoon, six men from Roseville, including the livery owner, came to the Inn. As it turned out, the ruffians made the livery owner feed and brush their horses while they were inside drinking. Returning drunk, they would sometimes rough him up. He was never paid. The plan was simple,

"Outnumber the ruffians. Once they see all of you, they will lose their will to fight," explained Ranger.

"What if they come back with more ruffians?" asked one of the men.

"They won't. Escalating the situation will backfire on them and they know that. Once you stand up to them, others will follow you. It won't be long before every man in Roseville will join the fight against them. There is another reason they will not return. As you know, Eastward Ho is the main source of income for Grumpelton. If villages and towns on the East-West road fear that the ruffians will attack them too, they will band together and stop buying the cattle, causing economic devastation for the city. You don't have to worry. The ruffians will not come back."

The men agreed with Ranger, and started to set the plan in motion, immediately. That very evening, the ruffians came to Roseville. As usual, they went to the livery, then to the Inn. When they arrived, things were definitely different. The ruffians, five in all, were greeted by twenty men, Ranger, and GLAMDOR, waiting for them. One of the men, a muscular, middle aged fellow with yellow hair, spoke,

"You are not welcome here! Leave, do not come back!" The ruffians grumbled and made a few threatening gestures. The men stood their ground with steely resolve. Seeing the determination of the Roseville men, the ruffians turned and scurried out the door. The livery owner was there with their ponies.

"That will be one-half silver piece each, for the care of your ponies," said the owner.

"You can't be serious," replied one of the ruffians in a surly voice, "they were with you for only a few minutes. You did not have time to feed and brush them."

"The fee is for all the times in the past you never paid me!" his words sounding firm and confident.

The ruffians looked at each other, trying to decide whether to pay him or not. The Roseville men came out of the Inn and surrounded the ruffians.

"You better pay him if you know what is good for you," said the yellow-haired man. They paid, mounted their horses, and galloped out of Roseville.

Back at the Inn, there was good cheer. The wife brought out flagons of ale. The men were proud of themselves. It was a long time since they had stood up for themselves. Over the next several days, hope spread throughout Roseville. Pride returned to the village. Beauty and Grace would soon follow. The plague never again would appear in Roseville.

Chapter 23

Jack's Temptation

Thus far, Jack's travels north had been uneventful. After leaving Squeak, he traveled several days north on the ND (Norland-Di-Wal-Nach) road. Having traveled on it before, he was familiar with many of the villages and smaller cities. The pandemic had infected only a few families. His main concerns were other travelers, wild animals, and the occasional bandit. However, he knew how to avoid danger, either by hiding, or by his guile. As an experienced traveler, he also knew it was best to keep his purpose to himself. When asked where he was going, he would reply, "To the capital of Norseland," but offered no other information. He was a fortnight south of the capital when he encountered an old man dressed similarly to Alvar, wearing a brown robe and sporting a long gray beard. They had stopped at the same place to water their horses. The old man was riding a dapple-gray mare. Her legs and rump were dark gray with light gray spots. The body, neck, and head were just the opposite, light gray with dark gray spots. Jack was riding a buckskin gelding. His horse's body was tan with black legs, mane, and tail. The two horse were wary of each other at first. After a few moments, the buckskin sauntered over to the mare and whinnied, which was horse language for "You are very pretty." She whinnied back, "And you are very handsome." The old man understood what the horses said to each other. He looked at Jack,

"Our horses seem to like each other."

"Really?" Jack asked quizzically. "How do you know?"

"Just a guess," answered the old man, not letting on that he could speak to horses. He then asked Jack,

"Where are you going?"

"To the capital city," Jack answered.

"Well, what do you know about that. I am too!" said the old man. "We can ride together. I think the horses would like that."

"Perhaps," Jack replied, not wanting to commit to riding a fortnight with someone he did not even know.

"It is settled!" said the old man, slapping his knee. "Let's get going. We have a long way to go."

They mounted their horses and headed north. For the next league, they rode in silence. Finally, the old man asked Jack, "What takes you to the capital?"

"A friend," Jack answered, not wanting to divulge his purpose. It was somewhat true that he was going to visit a friend. To be completely accurate, he had never met Talgor, but his daughter, Raven, was a true friend, which made her father sort of a friend. Moreover, it was Raven's prophecy that Jack and Talgor together would eradicate the pandemic from the north, which meant he and Talgor would certainly become friends, eventually.

"And you?" asked Jack, "why are you traveling there?"

"The same, to visit a friend."

Neither spoke for another league.

"I forgot to ask back at the stream, what is your name?" he asked Jack. For some reason that flew in the face of his traveling philosophy to not provide information, he answered, "Jackson, from the Kingdom of Ra-tan, go-gan, me-can, su-lan, and Maxfield."

"I thought so," said the old man. "Pleased to meet you. I think we have a mutual acquaintance."

"Who!?" asked Jack.

"The Wizard."

Jack was shocked! "How could this old man know that I know Alvar? Had he spoken to Alvar? When did THAT happen?" Jack thought to himself. It took another mile of riding before he could say anything to the old man. Finally, he asked,

"Who are you? How did you know I know Alvar? What else do you know about me?"

"I know you are traveling to the capital city, for what purpose I know not. How did I come by this knowledge? A raven came to me in the night three days ago. It was sent by Alvar, who asked me to travel with you."

"Why are you to travel with me?" questioned Jack.

"That I know not, also. I only know what the raven told me."

Jack had not been careful. It was he who had mentioned the name "Alvar". The old man was sly. He had an ulterior motive.

For the remainder of the afternoon, as they rode, they made only small talk, such as the weather, how far to the capital city, and the obstacles that lay ahead of them on the ND road. The biggest danger was the Red River Rift. Fortunately, there were no fell beasts there. The biggest danger involved crossing the Red River. Man-eating alligators lived in the river. One, in particular, was known as "Red Eye", because it had only one eye. As the tale goes, Red Eye had followed a canoe across the river, in which were a man and his son. When they reached the other side, the boy stepped out, and just as he did, Red Eye lunged out of the water and swallowed the boy whole. The father thrust his paddle into the alligator's right eye. He could not save his son, but he did blind Red Eye. That is why people say, to this day, "Always stay on the alligator's right side".

Jack and the old man did not have a canoe. They had to pay a ferryman to transport them to the other side. Jack spotted Red Eye following their flatbottomed ferryboat, which could hold as many as four horses and their riders. "Is that Red Eye following us?" asked Jack. The ferryman replied, "It is. Some passengers refuse to pay me. I wait until we are midstream, then knock them overboard. The ferryman had a very large pole he used to propel the boat. He lifted it out of the water and swung it at Jack, demonstrating how easy it would be to knock him overboard. As the ferryman lifted his pole out of the water, Red Eye rushed up beside the boat, nearby where Jack was standing, ready for lunch.

"Good thing we paid you!" Jack yelled.

Just as the old man and Jack were riding away from the river landing, a boy on horseback came galloping straight toward them, waving his arm over his head and shouting, "Grandfather, Grandfather!". He rode up, bringing his horse to an abrupt halt.

"Grandfather!" he exclaimed, short of breath, "Father sent me to fetch you. You must come now! Alone! It is not safe to be on the road."

"What is the matter? Why the urgency?" asked Grandfather. The boy replied, "Father did not tell me. He said only that I was to tell you to come back to the farm immediately, alone!"

The old man looked at Jack, then back at his grandson, and asked, "What about my friend here?"

"Alone! Alone! Father said you were to come alone!"

The grandfather looked at Jack, thought for a moment, then reached into his pocket, took out a brooch and handed it to Jack. "Jack, follow that one," pointing to another trail east. It will take you to my cousin's farm. Give him this brooch. He will care for you until it is safe to travel."

The grandson and grandfather rode away in great haste. Jack spurred his buckskin, following the trail east. The farm was not far, but there were several small rises and dips in the terrain, making the farm hard to see from the ND road. Upon arriving, he was greeted by three beautiful young women. They giggled and laughed at the sight of such a handsome man.

"Have you lost your way?" the blonde, who was obviously the oldest, asked. "I am Grethe," (pronounced greet ah) she said, with a gentle smile.

"I was sent here by an old man who said to give you this," Jack replied, returning her smile, and handed her the brooch.

Grethe took the brooch in her hand, examining it carefully. "Mmmm," she murmured. "Fleurine," she said, handing the brooch to her sister, "take this to Father." The girl rushed off to the house, brooch in hand. Grethe looked at the youngest sister, Bettina

(Bet tea na), and flashed her a knowing wink. Bettina winked back. Jack noticed the winks, which made him suspicious. But before he could act, Grethe took the buckskin's reins and led the horse, with Jack still in the saddle, up to the large Victorian house. By the time they arrived, which was at least a furlong more, Fleurine and her father were waiting on the porch.

"Welcome, good sir," the father said. "As a bearer of this brooch," which the father held up for Jack to see, "you are welcome to our home and all it has to offer." The three girls giggled. Jack wondered exactly what *that* meant. In time, he would find out.

The girls helped him off his horse and ushered him inside. They fussed over him, bringing tea and cakes for everyone. "Father has an herb garden behind our house. He grows special spices which we add to the tea. I hope you find the flavor to your liking," said Grethe. The tea was very good. It warmed and relaxed Jack. He was beginning to feel comfortable. His life over the last several months had been strenuous. This was the first time, in a very long time, that he actually felt some semblance of pleasure.

The sisters cooked a fine dinner, while Jack and the father chatted about why it was necessary for Jack to stay there. "There is great distress between here and the capital city," he explained. Bands of men are roaming the countryside, robbing and even pillaging, so I am told. It is not safe to travel. You are welcome to stay here until the garrison from the capital city establishes peace and order."

Jack had not eaten such an elegant dinner in many months, especially in such a fancy house. The evening was spent at a card table, where Jack seemed to always win. That night, he slept wonderfully in a comfortable bed for the first time in months.

The following morning, Bettina (the youngest daughter) brought Jack breakfast in bed. She served a tray full of fresh fruit, eggs, bacon, toast, coffee, even a cinnamon roll. He could not believe his good fortune. Life was good, thought Jack.

He lingered in his comfy bed, enjoying breakfast and the fact that he did not have to spend the day in the saddle. After dressing, he went down to the drawing room. Grethe was there, reading a book. "Am I interrupting?" he asked.

"No, not at all. Come, sit," she said.

Jack had not yet met their mother or any hired help, for that matter, on the farm. He was curious but hesitated to ask. Now, he felt, was a good time to ask.

"Tell me, Grethe, where is your mother? I have not met her yet."

"The pandemic took my mother two months ago, along with my brothers and all the other men. We have no one to run the farm after Father passes on. He too, has the virus. We don't expect he will survive."

It dawned on Jack that he was being enticed to stay on and run the farm.

He thought to himself,

"I have had a difficult life as a wanderer, searching ancient scrolls, fighting fell beasts, sleeping on the hard ground. Here is my chance to live a pleasant life. If I stay here, I would be rich, perhaps marry one of the daughters, and have two other lovely women to wait on me. I would live out my life in comfort and pleasure. Why should I leave? Why should I risk my life for some cause that will save the Middle World? What do I care about that? I have everything I need and want right here. "

The word WANT stuck in his head. He asked himself, "Is this what I WANT? Do I really want to live the rest of my life here?" He realized that as pleasant as the farm could make his life, what he really wanted was to be with Rae. His feelings for her were what mattered the most, not just a pleasant life. He could not stay! His destiny was to save the Middle World and marry Rae, not stay there.

"Grethe," his words were serious, "I cannot stay. Destiny is taking me in a different direction. As much as I want to stay, I cannot."

Tears welled up in her eyes. "Please don't go," she begged. "I am afraid we will not survive without you. We need you here, now."

At first, he sympathized with her sadness. But after a moment, he realized it was not exactly sadness. She hadn't known him long enough to care for him as a treasured person. She simply needed a man around to help them out. Any man! He looked deeper into her eyes. As he did, he saw it. THE VIRUS! She was infected! It all made sense to him, now. The entire family was infected. The father was not dying. He simply wanted a man to work the farm, as did his daughters. Jack felt the presence of evil. He knew he had to leave.

Assessing the situation, he saw an opportunity to leave AND bring Beauty and Grace to the family as well.

"I want to survey the farm," Jack announced. "Can you show me?" he continued.

She was delighted to show him, thinking her tears had persuaded him to stay. She dressed in riding clothes Jack wore his traveling clothes. Fleurine had cared for Jack's buckskin the night before. She had even braided his mane and tail. They began riding south, then turned eastward. At the eastern border, they rode north, following the farm's boundary, which was a small stream. Jack's plan was to ride the boundaries until he was closest to the ND road. At the northeast corner of the farm, they headed west, heading towards the ND road. At the northwest boundary, the closest point to the ND road, he said,

"I'm hungry. Shall we stop for lunch?"

Bettina had prepared sandwiches and their father's special tea. "Grethe," Jack began, "I cannot stay here. My destiny calls me elsewhere."

She pleaded with him to stay. "Your life here, on the farm, will be pleasant and prosperous," she said.

"It is not necessarily me who needs to be here. It is a man, any man. Grethe, you are infected with the pandemic. You and your sisters and your father. It has led you to believe that you cannot run the farm without a man. Grethe, that is NOT true. Within you and your sisters, is the power to overcome this disease. Once done, you will not need a man!"

Grethe was silent for several minutes as she considered Jack's words. Down deep, she knew they were true, but evil had convinced her otherwise. She began to disagree with him, but Jack held up his hand and said,

"That is not you talking. It is the pandemic. You know I speak the truth. You know true happiness will come from within you, not from a man."

Tears began to flow again down Grethe's cheeks. This time, however, they were real. It had been months since she last felt her power. She felt enlightened. She looked into Jack's eyes, "Thank you," was all she said.

Before he left, there was one more question that needed an answer.

"Grethe, did the old man have a part in our meeting?"

"Yes," she replied, "we gave him the brooch and promised him gold if he would send us a man."

"Then there is no danger on the road?" Jack asked. "No danger," she replied.

He mounted his buckskin, looked down at her and said, "Don't worry, your family will prosper, and joy will return."

Jack rode west to the ND road. She watched him ride off. Her heart and mind felt hope. She began to experience the feelings of Beauty and Grace.

Chapter 24

Ian

Evil, as Jack discovered, comes in many forms. The fell beasts in the Great Rift Valley were one form. The men waiting to attack the travelers at Grumpelton was another. Fear in Roseville was a third. Most recently, was temptation. Ian, Talgor's brother, had experienced evil in yet a different form. It happened during his ritual of Nach-Ny-Don-Qua.

Ian's Nach-Ny-Don-Qua, as with all boys about to enter manhood, was to spend three days and two nights alone in the forest with only the clothes on his back, a knife, and his wits. Like his brother Talgor, he was royalty. Unlike his brother, Ian was careful and thoughtful. He would not act first, then figure out what to do. His nature was to figure out what needed to be done first, then act.

In preparation for his ritual in the forest, he wore clothes that would keep him warm and dry, yet not heavy or cumbersome. His knife had a secret pocket in the handle. In it was a flint for starting campfires, a small piece of beef jerky, and a fishhook with line. He had a compass built into the top of the handle, so he would not get lost. He also decided that four men should escort him. He chose each one carefully. He selected the Captain of the Royal Guard, a military hero. The second was the wisest man in the kingdom. Third was the seer, who foresaw future events. And, finally, Ian's uncle, the King's brother. Ian's uncle had taken a special interest in him as a young boy. They spent many hours together, as the King's duties prevented him from spending much time with Ian. He wanted to get advice from all four men, before he began his ritual.

They accompanied Ian south from the capital city, down the ND road. Three leagues above the Red River, they rode west, to the "Woods Without Remembrance". The party set up camp there for the night, where they would remain until Ian returned. After dinner, the men shared stories of their own Nach-Ny-Don-Qua experiences. They told Ian of other life experiences also, some good, some difficult, some scary. The wiseman recalled words he once had heard from a much older and wiser sage:

If you tell me, I will hear,
If you show me, I will see,
If I do, I will learn.

"Doing," said the wiseman, "is the best way to learn".

Ian had spent much of his life hearing and seeing. "Doing" came after careful thought. He had planned, as best he could, for his ritual. The time had come to "Do".

The following morning, he bade his escorts goodbye, and walked into the forest. Using his compass, he navigated west for half a league, when he came to a small river. He saw a school of trout.

"Ah," he thought to himself, "dinner." Taking out his hook, line, and a bit of beef jerky, he sat by the stream and fished. The fish did not seem interested in his bait.

"Perhaps you should try this," a voice from behind him said. Surprised, Ian turned to see a badger with a handful of worms. "I will tell you what," said the badger, "I will give you my worms, and we will split whatever you catch." Ian considered the proposition, then said, "Agreed." By the time two hours had passed, they each had four trout to eat. "Been nice fishing with you," said the badger, as he took his trout and scampered off.

Ian was alone for only a few minutes, when a bear wandered by. "What is that I smell?" asked the bear. "Trout," answered Ian. "Would you share some with me?" asked the bear. "Perhaps," replied Ian. Now, Ian was in a delicate situation. If he upset the bear, it might eat HIM. On the other hand, a bear could be a good ally.

"Tell you what," said Ian thoughtfully, "if we had some fresh honey to go with the trout, it would make a fine meal. I will share my trout if you bring some honey."

The bear thought about Ian's idea. It reasoned, "Honey WOULD make the meal tasty."

"A beehive is not far from here," said the bear. "Good," replied Ian. "Why don't you go get us honey and I will catch more fish."

This was the first time the bear had been exposed to "teamwork". It considered Ian's proposal, then told Ian it would be back soon. Off it went to the beehive. Ian had caught several more fish by the time the bear returned with honey.

"I will start a fire to cook the fish," Ian offered. The bear looked frightened. Bears, in fact animals in general, are afraid of fire. "I will take my fish, raw!" said the bear who grabbed a paw full and hurried away. Ian had a lovely afternoon with his fire, fish, and honey. He thought to himself, "Nach-Ny-Don-Qua is ok. I don't seem to be having any problems I can't solve."

After eating his meal, Ian settled down for the evening. He gathered more firewood and made a bed of moss that he had found on the forest floor. He fell asleep next to the warm fire. As he slept, a storm blew in from the east. The wind came first, then heavy rain. Ian had warm clothes, but the rain was drenching. The moss soaked up the rain like a sponge. He found himself lying in a pool of water.

Jumping up, water dripped from his jacket and pants. He tried to restart his fire, but the downpour was too much. Seeing it was useless, he gave up. Instead, Ian found a giant oak tree, with great branches full of leaves. He huddled at the base of the tree, which provided shelter from the wind and rain. He tried to go back to sleep but had no luck. The rest of the night was miserable.

By the time dawn broke, the storm had passed. Wet and cold, he tried to start a fire to warm himself. It took several attempts before he got it going. This time, he was going to build a fire that could withstand another rainstorm. He also had no intention of spending another cold, wet night exposed to another storm. He began collecting wood for his fire, and branches for a lean-to. Much of the day was spent building his shelter. He also caught more trout. By sunset, he had completed his shelter and had plenty of trout. It was a clear evening, no moon. Ian gazed at the stars.

"Who, who, who, are you?"
Ian heard sounds coming from a tree above his lean-to. His eyes scanned the tree, trying to find what was making that sound. He saw nothing, but heard,

"What, what, what are you?"
He looked harder. Still saw nothing.

"Why, why, why, are you?"
followed by,

"Here, here, here?"

Finally, he saw it, a great gray owl with head feathers protruding up like horns. Most noticeable were its piercing eyes.

Ian watched as it flapped its wings and flew down, perching on the edge of the lean-to. The owl was half the size of a man, with fierce-looking talons.

"What do you want?" asked Ian. "Fish," replied the owl.

Ian tossed it one, which it caught with one claw and began tearing it apart with its beak. After finishing its meal, the owl began to chant again,

Who, who, who, are you?

What, what, what, are you?

Why, why, why, are you?

Here, here, here?

Ian told the owl who he was and about his ritual.

"Ah, so," said the owl, "then you must be the human I have been seeking."

"Seeking?" questioned Ian. "I don't understand."

"I am your guardian. I will protect you and give my wisdom to you," he said, sounding very wise.

"I am not alone. Two others will join us. Beware, one will help you, the other will deceive you."

The great horned owl began to teach Ian the ways of the forest. It taught him which animals were kind, which were dangerous, and which he could learn from.

"The badger has many talents. You could learn much from it," the owl counseled Ian.

Ian had been sitting up in his lean-to, listening to the owl. Leaning back, he felt something soft and warm. Then he heard a screech,

"Watch out! You are squishing me!" Much to Ian's surprise, he was about to lie on top of a badger. It had snuck through the back of Ian's lean-to and had nestled next to him without his knowing.

"As I said," the great horned owl continued, "the badger has many talents. Not being noticed is one of them."

"How did you do sneak into my lean-to without me knowing?" Ian asked the badger. "I will teach you," it replied, "as well as many other things." The badger continued, "Like owls, we badgers are predators. Unlike owls, who can fly, we hunt our prey by sneaking up on them, then pounce. You must be aware of your surroundings, both above, for owls, and on the ground, for badgers." After they finished their teaching, Ian said to them,

"I am not a predator. It is not in my nature." The owl responded, "That is true. But you must learn the ways of predators, so you don't become their prey."

"Do these lessons apply to humans too?" asked Ian. "Yes," answered the badger.

Several hours passed in deep conversation about the way of the forest, animals, and people. The owl stopped mid-sentence.

"Look," it said to Ian, nodding to just beyond the campfire. The badger had risen up in an attack position, ready to pounce. Ian saw what they saw, a dark gray snake. It slithered over near him-. Longer than Ian by a foot, it hissed,

"I bring-ssss you-ssss wiss-some-dum-ssss."

It slithered closer, with its tongue flicking in and out of its mouth. It hissed again,

"Closer-ssss. Come-ssss closer-ssss."

Ian bent forward. The snake rose up next to Ian's ear. Then, faster than the blink of an eye, it bit him on his neck, leaving two puncture wounds.

"You poisoned me!" exclaimed Ian.

"Not poison-ssss," it hissed, "a lesson-ssss. Caution first-ssss. Trust must-ssss be-ssss earned!"

With that, the snake slithered away. Ian reached up to his neck, feeling the wounds, two small holes from the snake's fangs.

"Those puncture wounds will be with you all your life, Ian," said the badger. "A reminder of what the snake said, 'Caution first, trust must be earned'."

"Why did the snake have to bite me? It could have just told me." The owl replied,

If you tell me I will hear,

If you show me, I will see,

If I do, I will learn.

"I understand," said Ian, "words would not be enough. The scars will always be a reminder."

The next morning, Ian returned to his four companions. Using his badger trick, he snuck into the camp unnoticed. He was there for several minutes, listening to the conversation before he showed himself. The men were surprised at his sudden appearance.

"How did you do that?" the Captain asked. "A badger taught me," replied Ian.

Examining Ian's neck, the seer said, "I see you met the snake."

"I did," replied Ian.

"I foresaw it would teach you to trust. You will need that lesson soon."

The party broke camp and returned home.

Jack had learned evil can come in the form of deception. Ian had also learned a valuable lesson. The snake had taught him not to be too trusting. His puncture wounds would be a lifelong reminder.

Ian was entering into manhood!

James Black

Chapter 25

Norseland

As Jack traveled north on the ND road, he was contemplating how evil comes in so many different forms. One of those forms, deception, was a form he had not experienced before. From now on, he would be more watchful. He worried that there were probably more forms of evil he had never been aware of. Time would tell.

The journey after visiting the farm was relatively uneventful. There were no dangerous incidents along the way. He simply rode his buckskin north. The road did pass up and over a few small mountains, some steep, but nothing compared to the steepness of the Silver Mountains. The road climbed through the last mountain pass, with snowcapped peaks on each side. When Jack reached the top of the pass, he looked east, seeing an expansive valley below. A winding river flowed through it. In the middle of the valley was a hill atop of which was the capital city. Fields of grain and tall grass surrounding the city waved in the wind. Villages dotted the entire valley.

Jack navigated the buckskin down the pass, through the valley, and arrived at the city gates.

"Who be ye, an whaaa da ya want?" sputtered one of the gate guards in a surly tone. Jack gave him his formal name,

"I am Jackson from the Kingdom of Ra-tan, go-gan, me-can, su-lan, and Maxfield. I have a message for your King."

"Who be ah send-n dat mess-age?" the guard again speaking in a rude tone of voice.

"That is not for me to say," replied Jack, in a confident manner.

The guard grunted, looked at the younger guard standing next to him, and said,

"Take dis fell-a to da palace. An be quick ta re-turn heeeere. No visit-n dat gurle yer sooo fond ah."

Jack followed the young guard through the winding and confusing streets of the city, arriving at the palace gates. He spoke quietly to the palace guard, then departed. The palace guard motioned for Jack to dismount and follow him. A stable boy led the buckskin away. Jack and the guard passed through a gravel courtyard, into the portico and through the massive double doors, carved with an ornate drawing of Talgor slaying a dragon. They were met by a royal secretary, dressed in a ruby red robe, with white trim. The palace guard spoke quietly to the secretary, who was looking at Jack, inquisitively.

"You have a message for Talgor? Who sent you?" asked the secretary, whose speech was articulate and sophisticated.

"Yes. I have a message for Talgor from his daughter, Raven," answered Jack in a matching sophisticated tone.

"Come this way," said the secretary. Jack was led into an ornate drawing room. There were paintings and sculptures of dragons, men with golden swords, and maidens dressed in battle regalia.

"This is the Dragon Slayer room," said the secretary. "You may wait here."

Jack took his time carefully examining the paintings and sculptures. He was impressed with the excellent artwork. One of the smaller dragon sculptures looked so real, that Jack was hesitant to touch it, for fear it would bite him. He had waited over an hour when a servant entered carrying a tray of tea and hors d'oeuvres. She set them on a table, then quietly departed. Another hour passed. Normally, one might be upset waiting two long hours. Jack, however, had traveled so many days and leagues to convey the message from Raven, that a two-hour wait was not disturbing to him.

Finally, a man entered the drawing room. "You are Jackson from the Kingdom of Ra-tan, go-gan, me-can, su-lan, and Maxfield?" asked the man. "I am," replied Jack.

"I am Ian, brother of Talgor, who is away. You can give Raven's message to me." Jack hesitated. He remembered Raven's words:

Jack, you will travel to the north. Find Talgor. Give him this ring, which he gave me when I left to become Alvar's apprentice. Tell him to locate and tame the Rainbow Dragon. Together, you, Talgor, and the Dragon will drive evil from the land. The north will then be free from the pandemic. Songs will be sung of your great deeds by many generations to come.

She had not mentioned Talgor's brother. Jack wondered if Ian was infected with the pandemic. "Is this evil being deceptive? Should I show the ring to Ian?" thought Jack, remembering his most recent encounter with evil at the farm.

Ian noticed Jack's hesitation. It reminded him of the snake's words, "Caution first, trust must be earned."

"Perhaps you would prefer to wait and speak directly to Talgor?" Ian offered, giving Jack time to consider what to do.

"When will Talgor return?" Jack asked.

"I cannot answer with certainty," replied Ian, not wanting to divulge too much. "After all," Ian thought, "this fellow, Jackson, might be infected. I should be cautious."

Nothing was decided at that time. Ian arranged for Jack to stay in one of the guest apartments, while they waited for Talgor to return. The apartment made Jack uneasy. "Was this another of evil's deceptions?" he asked himself.

For three days, Jack waited. For three days, Ian and Jack observed each other. They ate lunch together every day, each one watching for signs of evil. Late on the afternoon of the fourth day, Talgor returned. Ian greeted him with the news of Jack's arrival and message.

"What was the message?" asked Talgor.

"He will only give it to you."

"Well, let's meet this Jack, and hear what he has to say." With that, Talgor (who acted first and thought about consequences afterwards) went directly to Jack's quarters.

"Jack!" Talgor exclaimed, "I am Talgor. My brother says you have a message for me!"

Jack, still suspicious, asked Talgor, "What did you give your daughter when she left to become Alvar's apprentice?"

"A ring."

"This ring?" Jack asked, handing the ring to Talgor.

"Yes! How is she? Tell me about her! First, what is the message?" Talgor asked.

Jack told him he had traveled with her, Alvar, and others, to the Valley of the Unicorn. He recounted some of their experiences, including their trek through the Great Rift Valley, although he left out the scarier details. He told Talgor and Ian of Raven's encounter with the Unicorn. Finally, he gave Talgor the message.

"Well, then!" Talgor exclaimed. "Let's go find that dragon!"

Ian suggested they find out more information about the Rainbow Dragon before seeking it out. Naturally, Talgor wanted to leave immediately, but Ian was insistent.

"I will arrange for the trip," Ian offered, "while you seek out the location of the Rainbow Dragon, brother. Jack, our learned sages can tell you what they know of the Dragon."

Jack was taken to the palace library, where he was introduced to Vissodin. Her name means "wisdom of Odin". Odin, as everyone knows, is the greatest of the Norseland gods. Vissodin, as a young girl, fell in love with the study of dragons and dragon lore. Her knowledge of all things dragon was known throughout Norseland.

Vissodin began by telling Jack the story of the Rainbow Dragon's birth. Very little was known of the dragon's parents, only that the dragon's mother lay her dragon egg in the Woods Without Remembrance.

One day, a young girl and her father were strolling in the woods, when she happened upon the egg. It dazzled with every color of the rainbow when the sun's rays shown on it.

"Look, daddy!" the girl exclaimed, "look at the beautiful rock."

Her father did not see the rainbow colors. He only saw a gray egg-shaped stone.

"But it shines all the colors of the rainbow. Don't you see how beautiful it is?" she asked.

He did not. She put it in her coat pocket. When they returned home, she placed it in her dresser bottom drawer. It remained there for several months, as she had forgotten about it. One night, after she had gone to bed, she heard a cracking sound coming from the bottom drawer. Opening it, she saw the egg had a crack. She watched as the crack grew wider. Then, the egg split in half and from it emerged a tiny dragon. It radiated every color of the rainbow. Within a week, the dragon grew too big to live in the drawer. It moved under her bed. The girl had been feeding it meat from the dinner table. Her mother became suspicious, noticing her daughter eating much more meat than usual and taking meat scraps to her room. After her daughter left for school one day, her mother went into her room. There, she saw the dragon under her daughter's bed. She shrieked in fear, running out of the room calling for her husband.

The parents caught the infant dragon and took it deep into the woods and set it free. They wanted to kill it, but were afraid other dragons might find out, come and destroy their home and their lives.

The girl was broken-hearted. She cried for days. Determined to find her dragon, she searched the Woods Without Remembrance for many weeks. When she finally found her friend, she (the Rainbow Dragon was female) was over ten feet tall, had wings that could carry her high into the sky, and was able to breathe fire. The dragon, which the girl had named "Bow", after her rainbow colors, was happy to see her friend. However, Bow was also angry about being left for dead in the woods by some adults. She hated humans but loved the girl who was there at her birth. In some ways, Bow thought of the girl as her mother.

Bow and the girl remained friends for the rest of the girl's life. When she grew too old and frail to go visit Bow, the dragon left the Woods Without Remembrance, never to return. Over the centuries, Bow grew to mistrust humans, to the point of breathing fire on any that approached.

This was the situation that Talgor, Ian, and Jack faced. How were they to "tame" this dragon? How would the dragon help eradicate the pandemic in Norseland? Before those questions could be answered, they would have to *find* Bow.

Chapter 26

Grumpelton's Salvation

While Jack was searching for the Rainbow Dragon and Rae was making her way south with the girl named Said, Raven, J, Ranger, and Alvar were still faced with the problem of Grumpelton. They had visited several villages around the city, bringing Beauty and Grace to them. Grumpelton remained badly infected, a den of evil iniquity.

"Sometimes," Alvar said, "evil must be rooted out with the sword." Glamdor chuckled to himself as he remembered when he was in Alvar's cave, how eager he had been to learn swordsmanship. How Alvar had tried to teach him patience. Finally, Alvar had given up and let him practice with a sword. He recalled lunging with sword in hand at the old man, and how quickly Alvar had swung around behind him, slapping his backside with his sword. He still remembered the stinging blow.

"Now," Glamdor thought to himself, "the roles have been reversed. I am the one who wants to avoid the sword."

Alvar suggested they gather men from the neighboring villages and take the town by storm. He wanted to root out the evil by force.

"Well," Glamdor said, "I am not sure how that demonstrates Beauty and Grace."

"It doesn't. Sometimes force is necessary, first."

Glamdor thought about that. Then he said, "I have an idea. It involves the *threat* of force."

"Tell us," Raven interjected herself into the conversation.

Here is what Glamdor suggested:

We could do as Alvar said and recruit men from the neighboring villages. Bring them to the outskirts of Grumpelton. Have them surround the city. The four of us will ride into the town square. That will attract a mob with evil intentions to confront us. I will draw Glamring, set its blade afire, and speak to them.

"What will you say?" asked Raven. "I have no idea," Glamdor said, with a twinkle in his eye. Like Talgor, I will think of something."

Alvar spoke, "If your words don't convert the mob, the men can attack from all sides of the city, forcing them to give up the fight or else face death!"

"Sounds like a plan. Let's get started," Glamdor said.

Each member of the company went in a different direction, recruiting men from the villages. To their surprise, many women wanted to join. Many of the men thought the women would be in danger and should not be allowed to go. Raven viewed women's participation as a blessing in disguise. She explained that women can disarm men when they feel angry and confrontational. Her words were persuasive. The company agreed, women would join.

When all was ready, people from the villages descended upon Grumpelton from all four directions. Escape from the city was impossible. The city's menfolk were outnumbered three to one. As planned, Glamdor and the other three rode into the town square. A mob quickly formed a circle around the square, trying to trap them. Men began cursing and threatening them. Glamdor rode his pony in a circle inside the square, looking directly into the face of each man. Returning to the center of the square, he drew Glamring from its sheath. The mob backed off, seeing the brightly flaming blade.

Glamdor spoke, "Men of Grumpelton, I bring you Beauty and Grace!"

The mob grumbled and cursed J, "We don't want you here! Get out!" a large man standing in front of the mob said, as he reached for the hilt of his sword.

"Please, listen to him," Raven begged in a kind and gentle voice.

The mob quieted down. Glamdor continued, Glamring still blazing,

"Each one of you has a choice. You can fight us and die! We outnumber you three to one."

Glamdor raised Glamring and circled it over his head, showing the mob that every exit was blocked with villagers.

"Or," Glamdor continued, "you can let us bring you prosperity and joy. You each can find your *OWN* Beauty and Grace."

"To hell with you!" screamed the large man. He lunged at J. Faster than the blink of an eye, Glamdor was launched from his saddle by Glamring, who smote the large man, splitting his skull open. Glamring's magical powers scared the mob to death!

"We don't want trouble," said a smaller man standing near the now dead large man.

"Wonderful," replied J. "Who is your leader?"

"We don't have anyone to lead us since the last member of the Grumpelton family died from the virus," said the smaller man.

"Well then," smiled J, "I suggest YOU act as leader until the town can elect one." Looking over at Alvar, Glamdor said, "Alvar can stay and help you."

Smiles began to form on many of their faces. The mob was becoming a calmer crowd, soon to be a peaceful gathering of citizens. Beauty and Grace were begging to be contagious.

Glamdor gave a satisfied grin, nodded, turned to Ranger and Raven, and said, "Our work here is done!"

Chapter 27

Cece

Raven had foreseen some of the events which were to come. When she and Glamdor were with the Unicorn, visions had come to her. She saw a great fire-breathing Dragon. On its back rode Talgor. She saw its flames scorching the earth. She saw panic and fear in the infected people's eyes. She saw Jack and another man (later identified as Ian) trying to comfort and heal the peoples of Norseland.

A second vision came to Raven. She saw Rae and a young girl sitting next to The Hammer on his throne. Joyful celebrations were taking place throughout the Kingdom of Di-Wal-Nach. Evil had been driven from the land. Songs and stories were being written in celebration of The Hammer and Rae, who had saved the Kingdom.

Raven's last vision was that of a great battle. It lasted a few days and took place just outside the capital city of the Eastern Kingdom. It was the last, and greatest battle of the war against evil. Men from Norseland, Di-Wal-Nach, Grumpelton, and other western villages fought in the battle. Many died. The vison did not reveal who lived and who died, only that evil was vanquished. The death of so many good men weighed heavily on Raven's heart. She hoped there was a way to avoid that battle.

Raven revealed her visions to Alvar. She asked, "Will they all come true?" Alvar replied, "Visions sometimes reveal what WILL happen. Other visions reveal what COULD happen. We never know which is which."

Raven, Glamdor and Ranger visited the remaining few villages that were still infected. Word of their exploits in Grumpelton preceded them. There was some resistance to Beauty and Grace in a few of the outlying villages. Evil was making a last stand. It was only a matter of time, however, before evil would be driven out of the western province. Villagers who were infected bragged they would stand up to "The Four" (as Ranger, Raven, Glamdor and Alvar would become known). But "The Four" (or three, if Alvar was still in Grumpelton) needed only to ride into the village for the braggarts to melt away.

In those villages, it was usually the children who came out first to see them. Glamdor and Raven handed out candy. Smiles grew on the children's faces. Soon they were besieged by more children, hands extended out for candy, hearts hungry for Beauty and Grace. Returning home, the children brought Beauty and Grace back to their mothers. A few of the mothers sought out Raven, speaking to her privately.

"How did you bring smiles to our children?" they asked Raven.

"Candy, then Beauty and Grace," she answered with her Graceful smile.

"What do you mean by Beauty and Grace?" the mothers often asked.

Raven would tell them this story to illustrate what she meant:

Once upon a time, there was a young woman named Cece. She was born with two pronounced characteristics ... curiosity and determination. Cece's village was much like yours. Girls in her village were raised to be good wives and mothers. Unfortunately for Cece, curiosity and determination were not what men wanted in a wife. She tried to curb her natural curiosity and control her determination. But trying to change one's nature only results in frustration. By the time Cece had reached her fourteenth year, she was very unhappy and lonely. One day, as she was alone in the forest just outside her village, she heard the sound of a mother owl.

The owl called to her, "Cece, why are you so sad?" she asked.

"I must not be a good person," she replied, "no one likes me. I will never find a husband to marry."

"Oh, but you ARE a good person!" asserted the mother owl. "Your curiosity and determination make you very special, unique, and most of all, *GOOD!*"

Cece thought about the mother owl's words. She had never realized that her unique characteristics were beautiful. She thanked the owl and started home, with higher spirits. On her way, she stopped by a girlfriend's cottage. The friend had an older brother, who had always wanted to get to know Cece better.

"Tell me about yourself," he said.

Much to her own surprise, the words that came out of her mouth were, "I am a very curious and determined girl."

Much to her surprise for the second time, he replied, "I am very pleased to meet a girl who is curious, determined AND beautiful."

They struck up a friendship, became close friends, and married when they became of age. They had many children, who were also curious, determined, and beautiful.

"The moral of the story," Raven said, "is to always be yourself. Let your beauty shine. Don't try to be what others want you to be."

Most of the women went home holding Raven's inspiring words in their hearts. They returned to their families, feeling freer and more joyful. They were, for the first time in their lives, feeling totally themselves.

Most of the husbands noticed their wives' joy. Most embraced it, finding THEIR own beauty in doing so. The pandemic waned. There were, as is always the case, a few husbands that took offense, demanding their wives remain their old subservient selves. A few of these men banded together, angrily seeking out The Four. Confrontation would follow, which never ended well for the husbands.

Raven would speak first, explaining that The Four had no intention of interfering negatively in their lives. They simply wanted to bring Beauty and Grace to everyone. Sometimes, the husbands heard her words. They wanted more knowledge about Beauty and Grace. Others were of a different mind. They were intent on killing The Four, which would of course spread fear throughout the village. Wives would return to submission out of fear.

Ranger would then speak to those husbands. He understood their concerns. He explained that a new order was coming to the Eastern Kingdom. New laws would prevent husbands from dominating, and especially harming, their wives. "Here," Ranger encouraged, "is your chance to be a leader in the new order. Other men will admire you and follow your lead." Ranger did NOT explain that he was the rightful heir of the Eastern Kingdom and would inherit the throne once the plague was over. It was too dangerous to disclose his true identity. The Regent Caretakers of the Eastern Kingdom would try to kill him, keeping the throne for themselves.

All but a few of the husbands heard Ranger's words and agreed with him about the new order. The remaining men were too infected with the pandemic to be saved. Glamdor knew this and pleaded with the men,

"Please," Glamdor said with concern in his voice, "listen to Ranger. His words are true."

With that, Glamdor drew Glamring from its sheath.

"You cannot continue as you are!" Glamdor spoke as a warrior. "You MUST accept the new order!"

For a few, Glamdor's warrior tone and Glamring's flames were enough to change their minds. For others, his words had the opposite effect, making them enraged. The virus had taken control over their minds and emotions. They fell upon Glamdor with rage and violence in their eyes. Glamring would swing in a great arc, cutting them in half.

Sometimes, for Beauty and Grace to flourish, death must come first.

Chapter 28

Confusion

"There are times," said Alvar, "when sense makes no sense. When what is seen is not what IS."

"You mean like Ranger?" asked Glamdor. "He appears to be an ordinary traveling man, yet he is the rightful heir to the throne of the Eastern Kingdom."

"That is one example," agreed Alvar. "There are many others. You, Glamdor, are one of those others. People in the Kingdom of Kambuka think you are merely a boy, son of Calvin. No one there has a clue that you are one of The Chosen."

"Why are you telling us this?" questioned Raven. Alvar answered,

After you left Grumpelton, I was approached by an old seer. Her hair was long and gray. Her fingers aged and bony. Her skin wrinkled with time. Her eyes pierced shockingly into my very being as if it were Glamdor's flaming sword. She spoke to me, but without words. I immediately saw a vision of what was going to be a happier future.

Our efforts here in the west, have also served to fan the flames of evil in the east. It knows of your and Glamdor's power. The virus is ravaging the other provinces. We must hurry if we are to defeat it and save the Middle World. Ravens must be sent to Rae and Jack, warning them of the necessity to hurry. Talgor and the Rainbow Dragon must leave Norseland and sweep down from their mountain lair, driving evil before them out of the land. Rae and The Hammer must lead an army north through the marshlands, blocking evil's southern retreat. We will drive east, forcing evil back into the sea.

Alvar continued,

The final battle will be at the gates of the Eastern Capital. The seer did not show me who will perish, only that evil will be driven into the sea. I was shown a vision of flames raining down from the heavens above the final battlefield. Many men were struck down and killed. The battle did not result in Beauty and Grace. It created grief and sadness. Yet, it DID also create Beauty and Grace. The evil plague was struck down and driven into the sea. Everyone was free from its devastation. Each person could choose to follow Beauty and Grace, or not. Alas, many did not!

Alvar sent ravens flying north and south to alert Jack and Rae to the necessity of acting with haste. Jack, Ian, and Talgor had located the Rainbow Dragon in the Ice Mountain far to the north. They were well on their way when the ravens arrived with Alvar's warning. After reading the message, they pressed their horses harder and faster. In Norseland, men rode horses, not ponies. Naturally, Jack approved, since he himself rode a buckskin. They rode all through the night and the following day. Their path followed the Ice River, flowing south from the Ice Mountain. It was late afternoon when they arrived at the foot of Ice Mountain. It was steep, with sheer cliffs and with many icy crags jetting out from its sides. Ian found a goat trail leading up the mountain. Jack wanted to camp at the foot of Ice Mountain, climbing it the following morning. Talgor, never one to hesitate, said he was not going to wait. The others could wait for his return. Ian, knowing Talgor would not wait until morning, volunteered to go with him. Rather than stay alone, Jack went too. They followed the goat trail which zigzagged up a steep ravine. At the top of the ravine was the entrance to the dragon's cave. The opening was just tall enough for the dragon to squeeze through. Talgor, being much smaller, could easily walk right through it.

"Wait here," Talgor whispered, not wanting to awaken the dragon. "I will go alone."

Jack and Ian were relieved to stay behind. It is NEVER a good idea to wake a sleeping dragon. Talgor, of course, did not worry about that. His plan, if you could call it a plan, was to creep inside the cave before the dragon woke. He was not sure why he wanted to be inside. It was just a "feeling".

"Bow," cried out Talgor, with confidence and friendship, "I am here!"

Silence.

"Bow, are you sleeping? I have come with a message," Talgor announced.

Silence.

"Bow, the girl needs your help!" Talgor exclaimed.

Suddenly, there was a mighty roar. The walls of the cave shook violently.

"Who are you to mention that name to ME!!?" thundered the dragon.

"It is I, Talgor, dragon slayer, who has mentioned that name."

The dragon rose up on her hind legs, dwarfing Talgor. Flames hissed from both sides of her mouth as she shrieked, "You, of all humans, have no business in MY lair. I am going to burn you alive!"

"Before you do," Talgor said quickly, before flames could leave the Rainbow Dragon's mouth, "I have a riddle for you."

Dragons cannot resist riddles. Unfortunately, Talgor had not thought to prepare a riddle. He had to think quickly on the spot. Here is the riddle he posed:

You cannot touch or feel it

Yet it can kill you

It can make you do bad things

It spreads everywhere

Armies cannot conquer it

What is it?

Talgor added, "You have three guesses. What is your first guess?"

"Wind," answered Bow.

"Wrong! What is your second guess?"

"Snow."

"Wrong again! What is your last guess?"

"Heat!" exclaimed Bow, more of a guess than an answer.

"Wrong! Shall I tell you the answer?" Talgor said, knowing he had defeated the dragon.

"Yesssssss," hissed Bow.

"I will tell you. But if I do, you must grant me one wish. Do you agree?"

Poor Bow. She wanted to know. But she was frustrated that she had not guessed the answer herself. Moreover, she hated humans with a passion. ALL. Except for the girl.

"Oh well, granted. Now TELL me!" she demanded.

"EVIL"

There was a moment of silence as Bow thought about that answer. She thought about how she hated humans. How the girl's parents forbade her to see

Bow. But then, Bow remembered how she loved the girl.

Talgor, sensing Bow's conflict, spoke, "Evil has invaded, it has infected the girl's descendants." He paused for a moment, giving Bow time to recall her fond memories of the girl. Talgor knew Bow would want to protect the girl's family. He continued, "My wish is that you help me eradicate evil."

"Granted!"

Jack and Ian, who had been eavesdropping, gave a collective sigh of relief. They had been spared.

Bow emerged from the cave, followed by Talgor. He climbed onto the Rainbow Dragon's back. Looking down at his brother and Jack, he said, "Are you just going to stand there? Climb up here, we have a world to save!"

Bow held out her front leg. She lifted it up high enough for the two to climb up on her back.

"Ready?" Talgor asked Bow.

With a mighty roar, she leapt high into the sky and flew south to confront evil.

Chapter 29

The Rainbow Dragon

The Rainbow Dragon's arrival in the Norseland capital city caused quite a commotion. Word quickly spread that Talgor, the dragon *slayer*, had become Talgor, the dragon *tamer*. Ian, shunning the limelight, began developing a plan to rid Norseland of evil. One of his first tasks was to send a livery boy north for the purpose of retrieving their horses. Ian knew how much Jack favored his buckskin and did not want it harmed or stolen.

Jack dispatched a raven to Alvar, apprising him of how Talgor had "tamed" the Rainbow Dragon. He did not mention anything about his temptation to remain at the farm. Strictly speaking, Bow was not tamed. She had agreed to help drive out evil. Once that was accomplished, her obligation to Talgor was fulfilled.

Ian's plan called for Talgor, Bow, Jack and himself to start in the north of the Kingdom and work their way south. Talgor would ride Bow, swooping down the north side of each village. They were to circle the town or village and herd its citizens into the town square. Talgor and Bow were to land just outside the square. Talgor, still sitting atop the dragon, was to address them as follows:

> I have come to drive evil out of your lives. For some of you, my words will be enough. For others, more help will come to show you how to rid yourself of the plague. My brother Ian and his companion Jack will be here shortly. There are a few of you, for whom evil has rooted itself too deeply in your being to be helped. You know who you are. You may be feeling hate and violence towards me, and especially my words. Well, here are some words you will really hate.

> GET THEE GONE, EVIL!!

Following those words, the dragon was to rise up to her full height and issue a deafening roar and flames.

In a commanding voice, Talgor was to speak again,

> Leave! Cleave to evil if you must! Leave and never return! Run to your master. Serve it. But know this, your time will soon end. Evil will be driven out of the Middle World. You, who refuse to accept your Beauty and Grace, will die!

After Talgor finished speaking, Ian and Jack were to ride into the square on a wagon laden with food for a banquet. It would be called the Banquet of Beauty and Grace. Joy and happiness would abound. Friends and family would celebrate the end of the pandemic. There will be laughing, stories, and children running around with mouthfuls of candy. Naturally, lollipop soup would be a big hit with the children, who would grab the lollipops out of the soup and run off. After everyone's tummies were full, one or two of the elders would tell a story about life in the town before the pandemic. Then, families would disperse to their homes for a long and restful sleep. The first peaceful night's sleep for most since they were infected.

Ian knew that not all of the townsfolk would participate in the celebration. For them, the infection would not be cured by the dragon's roar, Talgor's words, or a feast. Some could be cured, in time, just by being in the presence of Beauty and Grace. They would participate in Ian's banquet, but not joyfully. And then there were a very few, who could not be cured. Talgor's admonishment was intended for them. Knowing they could no longer live in the presence of Beauty and Grace, they, according to Ian's plan, would slip away from the banquet, pack their belongings, and head south. The infection would have consumed their entire being, heart, soul, and mind. They would seek out others who were likewise infected. Driven to the southern border of Norseland, they would make their stand against Talgor and the Rainbow Dragon.

As Ian's plan was being implemented, Rae and Said were still on the ND road traveling south. It was never safe for two women to travel alone, especially with many men infected with evil. Rae and Said sought out families to travel with. Unfortunately, they were few and far between. They were only five leagues from the Di-Wal-Nach frontier when they encountered a group of men traveling in the opposite direction. The men stopped Rae and Said, forming a circle around them. Rae remembered being encircled by fell beasts in the Great Rift Depression. "It would be a good time for The Hammer to appear," Rae thought to herself. Alas, The Hammer did not appear. The men tightened the circle. One of them reached out to touch Said's shoulder. As he did, he said, "My, but you are a lovely girl." Rae pulled out her knife and slashed the back of the man's hand before he could touch Said.

"Ouch! You cut me!" he screamed in pain and anger. "I will make you pay for that!" he exclaimed. Rae's knife plunged into the man's right thigh.

"Try that again and I will kill you!" shrieked Rae. She began to turn in a circle, looking at each man directly. As she did, she asked, "Anyone else want to taste the cut of my blade!?"

The men backed off. Their injured companion limped away with the help of two other men.

"Thank you," the girl said, with an expression of relief. "You're welcome," Rae replied, with a smile. "We better not dally. Let's get to the border as soon as we can," declared Rae. They were careful to watch for other bands of men as they traveled the last few leagues to the frontier. Only once did they hear an oncoming band of men. Both women ducked out of sight and waited for them to pass.

Reaching the frontier, Rae explained that she had an urgent message for The Hammer. "Give us the message," said the border guard. "I will take it to him."

"I was instructed to give it to him personally," Rae replied.

The guard was not convinced. He insisted she give him the message, which he would deliver to The Hammer. This proved to be a dilemma for Rae. If the guard was infected, he would never take the message to The Hammer. She could not take the risk. Her options seemed limited. She could not use her knife. She and Said could not make a run for it. Her only option was the Raven Stone. Without saying a word, she drew it from the chain around her neck. Holding it up for the guard to see, she spoke, "It is imperative we speak with The Hammer." The stone's magic put the guard in a trance. He repeated her words, "It is imperative we speak with The Hammer." His eyes were glazed over as he spoke in a monotone voice,

"Take our horses. Ride south. You will arrive at dusk."

And so, Rae and Said did just that, arriving at dusk.

Chapter 30

The Wedding

Balwahahgishatoomi, (Bal Wah ah gish ah two me) the capital city of Di-Wal-Nach, (dye wall nach) was a name impossible for foreigners to pronounce. They simply shortened it to "To Me". The name, Balwahahgishatoomi, refers to the goddess who protects the city and its inhabitants. Her name was "Bal-wah-ah-gish", which means "Mother/protector of newborn babies". When a child is born, sacred incense is burned as an offering to her, insuring her protection of the baby. The last part of the city's name, "ah two me", roughly translates to "of our city".

When Rae and Said arrived at the city gates, Rae noticed the city was very tranquil. She asked the guards at the city's entrance, "Why?" They replied that a wedding had just been celebrated there, the previous day.

In fact, there had been a great wedding that lasted several days. It was the wedding of The Hammer and Laura.

Laura was born high up in the Silver Mountains, far above the Valley of the Unicorn. She, along with her brothers and sisters, were raised in a log cabin not far from the village of Woodcut. Pavelli

(The Hammer's birth name) had forged the Sharur of Garwalda in that very village. One day, Pavelli took a break from working at the forge and went into the village for fresh bread. He was about to cross the mountain stream when he saw a beautiful girl, her golden hair sparkling in the sunlight. His heart fluttered with excitement. Her beauty moved his soul. He *had* to know who she was! She happened to be returning home from the mountain stream with two full buckets full of water.

"Those buckets look heavy. May I carry them for you?" he awkwardly asked her.

She studied him for several moments before answering, wondering who this stranger was. She had never seen a young man with such a beautiful golden complexion. She was curious, wanted to know more about him, where he was from, and why he was in the Silver Mountains.

"Yes, please," she replied, handing him one of the buckets.

"Where are you from?" she asked with an inquisitive smile.

"Di-Wal-Nach," he answered, "far from here, where it is always warm, never snows, and no mountains."

"Why are you here?" she wanted to know.

"Here at this stream, or here in the Silver Mountains?" His answer conveyed he was not a simple man.

"Both," Laura wanted to know.

"I am in the Silver Mountains seeking my destiny. I am at this stream to meet you."

He was not exactly honest about why he was at the stream, but it was true he *had* to meet her. As they walked back to her home, she talked about her desire to travel. She would be delighted to see other lands, especially Di-Wal-Nach, where it never snowed.

It wasn't long before Pavelli became a frequent visitor at Laura's log cabin. Often, he would come for dinner and stay late into the night. The old man, with whom he was staying, was not great company nor a good cook. Laura had five brothers and sisters, all of whom met and liked Pavelli. By the time Pavelli had finished forging the Sharur, he was deeply in love with Laura. She had similar feelings, but was hesitant, for she did not know his future plans. One day, he took her aside and said with a heavy heart,

"Laura, the Sharur of Garwalda is finished. I must leave."

She knew that this day would come. The day he would leave to fulfill his destiny. Tears filled her eyes. Before she could speak, he continued,

"Laura, I love you! When I have finished what I have to do, I will return here, for you. If you will have me, I will take you to my country and marry you. But only if that is your heart's desire."

She smiled, with love filling her sad heart.

"My heart *does* desire you," her words choked with emotion.

"If you are willing, let us make an oath to each other. That we will remain loyal and unwed until we are together once again," said Pavelli.

And so, they did. Each swore an oath to remain loyal and unwed until they were together once again.

"Where will you go?" asked Laura.

"I only know that I am to be in the Great Rift Valley."

His departure was painful not only for Pavelli and Laura, but also for Laura's whole family. There were many tears and much sadness, for the entire family had come to love Pavelli like a brother.

It was almost a year before Pavelli returned. In the meantime, he had become The Hammer. He had saved the Circle from fell beasts and led them out of the Great Rift Valley. Having done so, he was now free to return to Woodcut and ask for Laura's hand in marriage. On bended knee, he took a ring from his pocket and asked her,

"Laura, will you marry me?" offering her the beautiful ring.

"I will have to ask my family if they approve," she said hesitantly.

They gave their wholehearted blessing, and she accepted his proposal. He then asked her to travel with him to "To Me", (Balwahahgishatoomi) where his family lived and where they would be married. The Hammer and Laura followed the ND road south. They had been on the road for only three days when they were waylaid by a gang of men. Pavelli tried to dissuade them from hurting Laura. One man, the gang leader, laughed at The Hammer, and pulled his sword. The Sharur of Garwalda flew from The Hammer's belt, striking the sword out of the leader's hand, catapulting it high into the air and far away.

"Are you The Hammer?" asked the gang leader.

"I am."

"Please forgive me. I did not know who you were. If I had, I would not have threatened you," the leader said in a pleading tone.

"If I *ever* hear of you or your gang harassing any other travelers, the Sharur of Garwalda will find you and disable each and every one of you."

Laura did not know the extent of her fiancé's prowess. She was very impressed, and was quick to tell him that, once they were out of the gang's earshot.

The Hammer wanted to slip into "To Me" unnoticed. His reputation was well known in the city.

Crowds of well-wishers would gather, beseeching him with requests for help. They waited until dark to enter. The Hammer wore a cloak, with a head covering. They arrived at his parents' house unnoticed. Joy and happiness filled the home. The wandering son had returned! Laura was immediately accepted as the "daughter-to-be". She was overjoyed by the prospect of being part of his family. The house was quite large. Many rooms, each furnished with paintings, sculptures, and gold shrines to their gods and goddesses. This was very different from Laura's log cabin.

The wedding took over a month to plan. There were invitations to send out, a banquet to organize, as well as creating two ceremonies. The first would be a formal and traditional Woodcut ceremony. The second would be the traditional one in Di-Wal-Nach. It was much less formal, and much longer.

Laura was exhausted when her wedding day finally arrived. Actually, it was not one, but three days long! On the first day, there was the traditional Woodcut ceremony. Laura wore a white dress, her head covered in a sheer veil. In her hands, she held a bouquet of fir bows and pinecones. Pavelli wore a black suit, with a bright red bow tie. Laura's brothers and sisters served as groomsmen and bridesmaids. It was a joyous family affair. Her father escorted her down the aisle and gave her to The Hammer saying,

"Love her with all your heart and soul and mind. She is yours to care for and protect."

The ceremony was short, in which they exchanged vows, rings, and were pronounced "Husband and Wife".

Following the ceremony was a banquet of traditional Woodcut foods. Venison, forest greens, loaves of warm bread, apples, and green tea. Black Forest cake was offered for dessert. It was a lavish meal with much joyous laughter, teasing, and storytelling. Laura's brothers told the story of how she, as a young girl, broke her arm. She was sledding, going dangerously fast, and crashed into a tree. From then on, they called her "Fearless LJ". L for "Laura", J for "jump" off the sled before you hit the tree. It was a reminder to be careful, which she was from then on.

After the meal, there was traditional forest dancing in which the dancers formed a line and danced in unison. The folk tunes were all fast, which tired out the dancers quickly. It was especially tiring for the Di-Wal-Nachers, who were not used to that kind of dancing. Everyone went to bed happy, with full tummies, and tired legs.

Day two was celebrated in the tradition of Di-Wal-Nach. It began with Pavelli coming early in the morning to collect his bride. Laura and her family were staying in a villa on the outskirts of "To Me". He was accompanied by all his family, friends, and a Silver Mountain goat, for Laura to ride. They made their way through the city to the Golden Temple of Galgahgalgish (Gal-gaw-gal-gish). Galgahgalgish was the goddess of marriage. As they traveled through the city streets, crowds formed to wish the couple well. It was the custom for the groom to throw candy to the crowd, which provided incentive to "wish the couple well".

After arriving at the temple, Laura and her entourage of women friends and family were escorted to the "preparation chambers". There, she was dressed in a pale-yellow strip of linen cloth. The cloth was wrapped around her body, from below her neck to her toes, fifty times. One turn for each year of happy marriage. Her veil was sheer, the same color as the dress. Her feet were adorned with diamond-studded sandals. On her fingers were four rings, one from her mother, one from her grandmother, as well as one from Pavelli's mother, and one from his grandmother. She wore a simple but elegant solid gold chain necklace. The Hammer wore the uniform of a Di-Wal-Nach officer. Around his chest was a red and white striped sash. Attached to the bottom of the sash was the Sharur of Garwalda. He was as handsome and striking as Laura was beautiful and elegant. Together, they were stunning!

Over one thousand people came for the ceremony, including Brother Obedient, the Wandering Priest, even the seminary abbot. It lasted four hours, during which many prayers, testimonies, and rituals were performed. There was a constant buzz of guests coming and going as the need for drink, food, and other necessities demanded they briefly leave the ceremony. Food and drink had been placed in the hallway just outside the grand hall where the ceremony was being performed. One of Laura's brothers went out for a drink of water. There were several men and women from "Me Too" chatting next to the drinks.

"Why is the ceremony four hours long?" he asked one of the older men.

"Suffering," replied the old man.

The brother did not understand. "I don't understand, why suffering?" he asked.

"Marriage is long-suffering. They'd better get used to it," replied the old man. He continued, "But living alone is worse. Better to share your suffering."

Following the ceremony was another feast. The cuisine consisted of delicacies from "Me Too", as well as other regions of Di-Wal-Nach. Dancing was less formal than the night before. Musicians played exotic music on their string and wind instruments, accompanied by a very large drum. People danced alone, in pairs, in groups. They let the music flow through them. It was very late into the night when the last of the revelers retired.

The third day began with the Wedding Breakfast. Pavelli and Laura, husband and wife, rose early to help prepare the food. There would be about fifty in attendance. Fortunately, there were several cooks and servers. As the guests entered the banquet hall in the Golden Temple of Galgahgalgish, they were greeted by the bride and groom's parents. Pavelli, The Hammer, wore a peasant shirt, and simple trousers. Laura was in a peasant dress. Both wore no shoes. Their humble appearance was to be a reminder for them to serve their fellow citizens with humility.

It was early afternoon by the time all the guests had eaten and departed. Laura and her new husband were exhausted, as was the entire wedding party. They all went home and slept until the following morning.

A wedding to remember.

Chapter 31

Cleansing

Alvar had sent a raven to warn Rae of impending doom. It found Rae the day before she and Said arrived at "To Me". Evil would infect Di-Wal-Nach if she and The Hammer did not act swiftly.

Talgor, the Rainbow Dragon, Ian, and Jack were driving the infected people south out of Norseland. These evil ones had already crossed Norseland's southern border into the Eastern Kingdom. If Rae and The Hammer did not act with haste, these people would continue south into Di-Wal-Nach, bringing with them the pandemic.

Up to this point, the plague had infected only a few people in Di-Wal-Nach. Its citizens were, by their very nature, filled with Beauty and Grace. Nevertheless, they still were not immune from an onslaught of badly infected Norselanders. These evil men (and a few women, too) would have to be kept out of the country.

Rae found The Hammer and his new bride, Laura, preparing to leave for their honeymoon.

"I am so sorry to have to tell you this," Rae's voice expressing urgency, "but the plague will soon infect all of Di-Wal-Nach if we don't act NOW!"

Laura especially, was not happy to hear this news. "We were just leaving for our honeymoon," she told Rae.

"Your honeymoon will have to wait!" Rae said firmly. "Evil will not wait until you have had your *honeymoon!*"

Laura understood Rae's urgency. "Then, in that case," Laura said with determination, "I am going too. I will accompany my husband NO MATTER WHAT!"

Rae could see arguing with Laura was pointless. "Alright," Rae agreed.

"What about me?" asked Said, in her young and innocent voice.

"Who are you?" asked The Hammer.

Rae explained who Said was and how the girl had come to travel with her.

"My family will care for you," The Hammer's voice was kind and reassuring, "they will help you, and make sure that you are educated and properly married."

Said had no intention of marrying, after experiencing her mother's abusive marriage. "Education, yes, marriage, NEVER!" exclaimed Said. The Hammer's family did help her obtain a fine education. It had always been her desire to establish a house for battered women. When she became of age, they helped her realize her dreams. It was named

"The House of Said". She found only a few women in Di-Wal-Nach who needed her support, so at the age of 25, she moved The House of Said to the village where her family lived. It became a refuge for many women. There, they were encouraged to find their own Beauty and Grace.

Laura, Rae, and The Hammer rode northeast, towards the border between Di-Wal-Nach and the Eastern Kingdom. Laura, who had not yet experienced fear like Rae did, when she was traveling in the Great Depression Valley, was excited and hopeful. Visions of saving the Middle World filled her mind. She saw all of them riding into the Eastern Capital as conquering heroes. Rae and The Hammer had a different perspective. They knew the difficult and dangerous road that lay ahead. For them, it was grim determination, not hope and excitement, that dominated their thoughts.

Their first encounter took place only a few leagues south of the frontier. A group of two dozen men and a handful of women had crossed the border into Di-Wal-Nach. They had already raided two small villages, burning and looting in search of food, money, and other valuables. In the distance, Laura saw the smoke.

"What is burning?" Laura asked.

Rae and The Hammer looked at each other. Although both suspected it was the work of evil, neither said a word. They rode on. Approaching the burning village, they encountered a band of men and women. Rae rode bravely ahead and addressed them,

"You have entered the land of Di-Wal-Nach. You are welcome to stay, if you are willing to rid yourselves of the pandemic."

One of the women, who was seriously infected, but weary of being on the run from Talgor and Bow, asked,

"How do we do that?"

"Beauty and Grace," answered Rae.

Those two words enraged the men. They drew their weapons and charged towards Rae with rage in their eyes. The Hammer drew the Sharur of Garwalda, raised it over his head and shouted "STOP!". A few hesitated, but most kept running towards Rae. The Sharur left The Hammer's hand, flying directly into the mob. It split them right down the middle, striking down several of the men. Laura saw that the Sharur had left a spider-like thread in its trail. Once on the far side, the Sharur made a spider web around the mob, as it flew in circles. The infected Norselanders found themselves trapped in the web.

Rae repeated, "As I said, you are welcome to stay if you want to rid yourselves of the pandemic."

The woman who had spoken before, asked again, "How do we do that?"

Rae held the Raven Stone over her head and shouted, "Follow me!"

Three women and two men were magically freed from the spider web. They walked over to Rae. She lowered the Raven Stone for each person to touch. They were cured. Smiles filled their faces.

"You have made your choice," Rae said with finality to the remaining mob, "You have forfeited your lives."

The Sharur of Garwalda had returned to The Hammer. He whispered to it. A lightening flash shot from the tip of the Sharur, setting the trapped mob on fire. All were destroyed.

"Go tell your fellow Norselanders what awaits them if they choose to remain with evil!" Rae instructed the two men and three women. The five fled north to spread the word.

Laura was stunned. She had never experienced violence and death. Like Rae and The Hammer, she now felt grim determination. Rae asked her,

"Do you want to return to 'To Me'?"

"No! I am here and will stay here with my husband!"

"So be it," Rae said.

Rae, Laura, and The Hammer continued on into the burning village. There, they tended to the injured. Rae and Laura were able to save several. The Hammer sought out the remaining men. He inspired them to rebuild their village and bring back Beauty and Grace. Each of the men touched the Raven Stone. Beauty and Grace had returned!

Laura, Rae, and The Hammer continued north, searching for more burned villages and infected Norselanders. When they entered a destroyed village, Laura and Rae would tend to the injured. The Hammer would assemble the men. As before, each man touched the Raven Stone. Each man would then begin to rebuild his family, his home, and the village.

When they would encounter a mob of Norselanders, Rae, and on occasion Laura, offered them the choice of cure or death. Word was spreading among the infected Norselanders faster than the disease. Rather than risk death, most returned north. Within a fortnight, virtually all of the Norselanders and infected Di-Wal-Nachers had been trapped in the Eastern Kingdom, between the Rainbow Dragon and the Sharur of Garwalda.

Both Kingdoms were cleansed!

They were free of the pandemic. Now, the time had come to free the Eastern Kingdom. It would come to be known as the "Battle of The Chosen"!

Chapter 32

Reunion

Rae, Laura, and The Hammer made their way north to the East-West road. They had already crossed the frontier into the Eastern Kingdom.

"We were to meet Alvar here on the road," Rae said, "but we don't know if he is east or west of us."

The Hammer smiled, then whispered to the Sharur of Garwalda. It flew out of his hand, following the road to the east. Soon, they saw it pass over them heading west. Finally, it returned to The Hammer's hand.

"Alvar is one day west of us," said The Hammer.

Meanwhile, Jack, Ian, Talgor, and Bow were coming from the north, driving out the infected people who had refused to accept Beauty and Grace. Two days after Laura and Rae, they arrived at the East-West road. Bow was sent to find Alvar. She returned with the news that she had found him in an abandoned village east of their location. They set out and within a few hours arrived at the village. Rae, Laura, and The Hammer had arrived the day before.

It was a joyful reunion. There were hugs all around. Raven leapt into her father's arms.

"Father!" she exclaimed, "I am so happy to see you." She smothered him with hugs and kisses. Then she turned to her uncle, Ian. He too was smothered with hugs and kisses.

"What about me?" Jack asked, looking at Rae. She took three steps towards him, then threw her arms around him, hugging and kissing him too, a little longer than the others.

Bow watch all the hugging and kissing with disdain. "Disgusting," she thought. Dragons don't approve of that kind of affection.

The Circle had been tightly bound together through meeting many adversities together. In their travels to and in the Golden Plains, the Great Rift Valley, Silver Mountains, and the Valley of the Unicorn, they had come to rely on each other. They came to appreciate each other's strengths and weaknesses. They were overcome with emotions, knowing that the circle was once again complete. But now, newcomers were there, too.

"Who is this?" asked Alvar, glancing at Laura.

"My wife, Laura," answered The Hammer.

"She must be something very special, for you to bring a woman on such a dangerous journey," Alvar said in a manly tone.

"Humm ....I see," replied The Hammer, "If this is so dangerous, then why did YOU bring women?

Why did you send Rae ALONE to find me? Why is the young girl Raven with you?"

"Touché," replied Alvar. "Pleased to meet you, Laura. I apologize if I was offensive," he said, realizing his error.

Laura graciously replied, "It is my honor to meet you."

Jack introduced Bow, Ian, and Talgor to the others.

Winston, not to be left out, brayed at the top of his lungs.

"Dear Winston," Glamdor said, stroking his neck, "we could never leave you out. You have been in this story longer than any of us. After all, it was YOU who brought Ponakwa to Kambuka long before we even BEGAN our journey."

Winston gave a satisfied bray, then nodded towards his grain bag. Glamdor took a heaping handful and held it out for the mule.

After all the introductions were made, Alvar declared, "First, we should eat, then make our plans."

The meal was simple but hearty, consisting of roast beef, corn on the cob, collard greens, baked potatoes, and bread. The food and drink (tea with honey and fresh spring water) had been a gift from the citizens of Grumpelton. Having recovered from the plague, they wanted to show their appreciation.

Alvar suggested having a "reunion" banquet for the Circle and guests.

During the meal, they teased and told revealing stores about each other. They teased Glamdor about always being hungry. Glamdor teased Raven about always being "right". They asked Talgor to recount how he became the "dragon slayer". Jack told of the Red River and the man-eating alligator. He did not mention his temptation at the farm. Rae told the story of how she met the young girl, Said.

After their tummies were full and their stories told, they formed a large circle with their chairs. Even Bow and Winston were part of the circle. Although, Bow was so large, she had to stand behind Talgor and Ian.

"The time has come," Alvar said in his most serious tone, "for us to deliver the final blow to the pandemic. We must drive it out of the Middle World."

There was a moment of silence as they considered what his words meant. The task facing them was full of unknown dangers. They would be risking their lives. Some of them might not return. Winston, who understood every word but refused to speak, brayed mournfully. Only Bow was happy, for this meant her obligation to Talgor would be met and she could return to her cave in Ice Mountain and take a long nap. A long nap for a dragon lasts centuries.

Raven had foreseen what was to come. Her vision, when she and Glamdor had met the Unicorn up on the mount, was of diseased people flocking to the Eastern Capital. She saw a great battle taking place. She saw flames from a dragon and death wrought by a Sharur. She saw a great funeral pyre. She did *not* foresee Beauty and Grace.

"We must drive evil to the Eastern Capital," Raven's tone was determined, but sorrowful. "There, I have foreseen, the "Battle of The Chosen" will take place. Death will reign over the capital. There will be NO joy!"

"It will be as you have foreseen, Raven," said Alvar, continuing,

We shall drive evil east! The Hammer, Laura, and Rae will sweep south, herding evil back to the East-West road. Jack, Talgor, Ian, and Bow will ride north, doing the same. The rest of us will form the main force, driving the infected east until their backs are to the shore. They will amass in the Eastern Capital, thinking they will be safe behind its walls. But they will be trapped. There we will deliver the final blow, eradicating the Middle World of the pandemic.

The gravity of the task before them settled in. They fell silent, each lost in his or her own thoughts. Although they went to sleep early, none slept well. Jack had a nightmare. He dreamt that Rae was captured and tortured. Trying with all his might, he could not get to her in time to save her. Glamdor dreamt of the "Battle of the Chosen", in which Glamring slaughtered hundreds. He felt great remorse in his dream for having caused the death of so many. Winston's dream was of Naomi making him into a pot roast for not bringing J, Naomi's boy, home safe and sound.

The following morning, breakfast was a somber affair. Few spoke, and when they did, it was small talk like, "Is your breakfast ok?", or, "Don't forget to pack warm clothing". After breakfast, they readied the ponies, horses, and Winston. Alvar appointed ravens to travel with the three groups. He said, "The ravens will guide us and alert us of danger. They will also deliver messages between us."

They gave each other a final hug, mounted, then rode off in their appointed direction.

The beginning of the end had begun.

Chapter 33

Raven's Paradise

"If I may ask," Ranger asked Raven as they rode east on the East-West road, "what kind of father is Talgor?"

She replied with a bittersweet smile, "He is 'Talgor, the Dragon Slayer'."

"That is true," pressed Ranger, "but what kind of *father* is he?"

Her eyes brightened. "He is *magnificent!*"

Ranger saw Beauty and Grace in her demeanor. She rose up in her saddle, riding taller, more graceful, with pride and purpose, as she continued,

He is a generous and loving father. He makes me feel important. He often tells me I am powerful, and one day, will have a great impact on the People of Norseland. He brings little gifts to me from his travels, as a reminder of his love for me. His charm is infectious. I can't help but smile when I see him charming others. By his example, I am learning about charm. He is fun. My father loves to be silly, to giggle, and be mischievous. I see joy in his eyes when he plays little tricks on me. He loves to tease me. His Beauty and Grace are inspiring. I want to be like him, in that way. I want my Beauty and Grace to blossom as his has, but in my own unique way.

"Ranger?" Raven asked, "tell me about you. I only know what I have seen in my visions."

"I don't think you will find me at all interesting," was his reply.

"If my visions are true, you are *certainly* interesting. Please tell me," her voice sincere.

"Well, if you really want to know," he answered, then paused before continuing.

Their ponies continued down the road at an easy pace. Alvar had advised them to ride slowly, giving time for the two other groups to take up their positions north and south of the road. The sky was partly sunny, dew still on the ground. The morning was cool, the air was still. Ranger told her,

The story of my family began long, long ago, when the goddess Brigina (bri gee na) chose to bring Beauty and Grace into the Middle World, by bearing a human child. Humans, at that time, were without purpose. Beauty and Grace did not exist. Once a year, she would visit the Middle World, searching for the man who would be her child's father. It took hundreds of years before she found Bram (burr am), meaning 'father of many'. Appearing to him in a dream, she divined he would fall in love with a 'golden-haired maiden', who would bear his children. During that summer, Brigina appeared to him in reality as that very maiden. He was smitten, and soon she was with child. The following spring, Brigone (Bree gone) was born. As a child, his Beauty and Grace were already apparent. He became a great sage, traveling throughout the Middle World, bringing Beauty and Grace everywhere he went. While in the land now known as the Eastern Kingdom, he fell in love with a beautiful woman. Soon after they were married, a male child was born, followed by seven daughters. Brigone continued his travels, but each spring returned to his family to celebrate the baby's birth, which was the birth of Beauty and Grace in the Middle World.

His daughters bore many children, each blessed with Beauty and Grace. His son, named after his grandfather, Bram, was a fierce warrior and great leader. He united all the tribes in the east, forming the Eastern Kingdom under his rule. He founded the "Royal House of Brigina", named after his grandmother, the goddess Brigina.

The Eastern Kingdom prospered under the House of Brigina. For a thousand years, Beauty and Grace reigned. It was during the time of the Great Queen, when evil spread, that the House of Brigina succumbed to the disease. The youngest daughter was taken into the Valley of the Unicorn, where it was hoped she would be safe from the plague. A Regency was established to manage the Eastern Kingdom, until the rightful heir could reclaim the throne. Ragbot (rag bought) was elected as the regent. He quickly consolidated power. By the time the plague ended, he had complete control over the Kingdom. Not wanting to give up his control, he sent agents to find and kill the sole House of Brigina survivor. Fortunately for her, she was hiding in the Valley of the Unicorn, where she was safe.

I am her last living descendant.

After listening to Ranger's ancestral history, Raven wondered aloud, "Why was I one of the "Chosen"? It should be YOU, not Glamdor and I."

"My role in this great adventure, is to restore the House of Brigina and rule the Eastern Kingdom, NOT to save the Middle World from evil. That is your and Glamdor's role," spoke Ranger.

"What, if I may ask, is your real name?"

"Bram," he answered, speaking with pride and authority. "As his descendant, I was named after the founder of the House of Brigina."

"Why then are you called Ranger, and not Bram?" Raven asked.

"The current regent, Ragbot's descendant, would have me killed if he knew of my existence."

"Then," offered Raven, "I shall continue to call you Ranger, until you ascend the throne."

"Thank you," Ranger said, knowing he could trust Raven.

Ranger and Raven had lagged behind Glamdor and Alvar. Rounding a bend in the road, they found them eating lunch. Winston was grazing with the ponies.

"Did you two have a good talk?" inquired Alvar.

"We did," replied Raven, shooting a knowing glance at Ranger.

"The next village is only three furlongs ahead," Alvar said. "A raven has returned to tell me there are dozens of men and half a dozen women there. They are all infected. I anticipate we will have a difficult time curing them."

"Should we seek help from the dragon or The Hammer?" asked Glamdor.

"No. You and Raven, as the Chosen Ones, have the power to cure," reminded Alvar.

After lunch, they rode into the village. As they suspected, they were met in the square by a mob of belligerent men and women. Raven began her usual plea to save themselves. But this time, a very angry man, not waiting for her to finish, drew his knife and threw it at Raven, striking her in the thigh.

"OWWW!" wailed Raven.

No sooner had the knife stabbed her, than Glamdor lunged off his pony into the crowd, striking the knife-thrower dead. Then, Glamring swung in a great arc, killing another six men and one woman. The mob backed away, fearing for their own lives.

"I suggest you hear Raven's words before any more of you die." Glamdor's voice was strong and commanding.

Silence fell over the mob. Alvar rushed over to Raven. Fortunately, she had been wearing buckskin breeches. Only the very tip of the knife had broken through and pierced the skin. She was bleeding, but only lightly. She appeared to be unaffected by the attack of the knife.

"Beauty and Grace," Raven began again, "can save you. As you just witnessed, your alternative is to face the wrath of Glamring."

Glamdor raised the sword high above his head. Its searing flames shot out in all directions. Once again, the mob backed away, fearing for their lives.

One woman, then a second one, stepped forward. "We want to be saved," said the first woman. Raven felt like she was staring evil in the face. Her words, which *sounded* sincere, did not ring true. She was lying. Raven saw the same evil in the second woman's eyes. She too, was lying. Raven drew her knife, dismounted, and approached the first woman.

"Are you sure you want to follow this path?" Raven queried the woman.

"Oh yes, I want "beauty and grace"," she lied.

In an instant, Raven's knife slashed her throat. She fell to the ground, gasping, and died. Addressing the second woman, Raven asked, "What do YOU choose?"

The woman hesitated. Raven could see she was fighting an internal battle between good and evil. A moment later, the woman's eyes hardened. Consumed with hate and rage, she lunged at Raven, arms extended with the intent of strangling her to death. Death, however, found the woman first. Raven's knife plunged into her heart. She fell dead on top of the first woman.

The mob was stunned. An eerie silence fell over the village square. After a few moments, feet began to move. Those at the back turned around, walking at first, then running away. Those at the front did not run away. With a wild scream, they attacked. The four were surrounded by several dozen enraged men. Suddenly, Glamring swung in a great arc, slashing arms, chests, and necks. Alvar's staff shot lightning bolts into the charging crowd. Ranger drew his sword and charged the mob. Ironically, it was Raven's knife that they most feared. Holding it in her hand, ready to thrust, the men standing in front of her backed away. The battle lasted only a few minutes. When it was over, many of the men were dead. A few had run away. Others were injured, lying on the ground. Ranger sustained a knife wound on his left arm. Glamdor had a small cut on his left leg. Alvar's magic had shielded him from harm.

Raven went to each of the injured men lying on the ground. "What is your choice?" she asked. Some did not want to die. On the other hand, evil had infected their minds, making the choice very difficult. Only a few chose Beauty and Grace. Raven placed her hand on the forehead and whispered into the ear of each man. Evil fled from the minds of some of the men. They rose, free of the plague. But most chose not to live. Raven's knife fulfilled their choice.

When it was all over, those who were still alive asked, "What shall we do now?"

Glamdor answered, "You have a choice. Either return to your homes or stay here and start a new life."

None wanted to return to the devastation of their former villages and cities.

"We will stay here and start a new life," one of the men said.

One of the women chimed in, "We shall name this village Raven's Paradise, for it was Raven who brought paradise to us!"

Chapter 34

Eastward Ho

After the skirmish at Raven's Paradise, Alvar dispatched several more ravens to scout out the area ahead. He did not want to encounter any mob, unprepared. They returned with the unsettling news that between them and the capital city of the Eastern Kingdom, was a small city with hundreds of infected men and women milling around in the streets. Alvar sent ravens to Jack and Rae, instructing them to come for a council meeting in Raven's Paradise. Additional ravens were also sent to the city in hopes of learning the extent to which the pandemic had infected the citizens. The ravens returned before Jack and Rae did, with news that there were more people than first reported. But being birds, and not humans, they could not determine the extent of the pandemic.

The council was held with the Circle, as well as Talgor, Ian, The Hammer, and Laura. Bow was also present. After much discussion, it was decided that more intelligence was needed. Glamdor suggested he and Raven go to the city by themselves. That way, it would be unlikely they would be perceived as a threat. Winston brayed three times. Glamdor walked over to him and whispered,

"Yes, Winston, Raven and I will certainly take you with us. You will be our protector," adding, "that way you won't end up as Naomi's pot roast."

Glamdor, Raven, and Winston made their way to the city. The others followed, making sure they were not seen. Often, they would have to rush off the road and hide. Bow flew north, keeping them in sight, but staying far enough away to not be seen by other travelers. As a dragon, it's not easy to hide. Nor is it in their nature to hide. Bow continued flying north, many leagues, finding a suitable mountain peak where she could see, but not be seen.

Raven, Glamdor, and Winston followed behind a group of farmers who were taking their produce to the city's market. Unnoticed, they mingled with the shoppers, listening and watching for signs of the virus. Right away, it became evident that the plague had infected most of the shoppers at the Farmer's Market. They left the market in search of the city square. The situation was the worst they had ever seen. The square was large, in disrepair, with broken benches, weeds growing everywhere, and overgrown trees. There were many groups of people, arguing not only within their own group, but also with other ones.

Glamdor stayed just on the edge of the square with Winston. Raven made her way to one of the groups. There was an argument over who was the rightful owner of a goat. The goat had a rope around its neck, and two men were tugging on it trying to get the rope away from the other.

"It is MY goat," shouted one of the men, "I raised it since it was a kid."

The other man angrily replied, "You stole it from my herd just after it was born."

Raven considered intervening, but decided it was best to not get involved.

One of the groups consisted of citizens from Norseland. They were talking about a dragon which burned people alive. One of the men in the group held up a burned hand, for verification. His wife corrected him, "You burned that in a campfire on the way here. We never even SAW a dragon!" The man looked at his wife with anger, then slapped her across the face. "Shut your mouth!" he exclaimed. Raven was shocked! The pandemic was worse here than she had imagined.

She returned to Glamdor and Winston. They continued their tour of the city, making mental notes of where and how many infected people lived there. Upon their return to the company, they reported that there were several hundred infected men angry enough to fight.

"Too many for us to fight without help," said Alvar, thoughtfully. "We must get reinforcements!"

"I have an idea," offered Glamdor,

Why don't we get Grumpelton to do "Eastward Ho"? They could drive the cattle into the city from the west, which would force the infected out through the eastern gate. There, we would be waiting. If we could muster up one thousand men from the villages and cities we have already cured, they would constitute an overwhelming force. Many of the infected would choose Beauty and Grace. Those who refused would be trapped.

"That sounds like an excellent plan," said Jack. "I agree," added Raven. There was some discussion and disagreement on the logistics of the plan. However, no one had a better idea. So, it was adopted. Alvar and Ranger rode back to Grumpelton. They organized the "Eastward Ho" drive. In the meantime, Glamdor, Rae, Laura, and The Hammer circled south of the city, cleansing small villages as they went. Raven, her father Talgor, Jack, and Ian went north doing the same. When words could not persuade villagers, Bow was summoned. Her mere presence was often sufficient to save an entire village. The two groups met on the East-West road, east of the city. There, they waited for Alvar, Ranger, and "Eastward Ho". As they waited, villagers who had been cured began to arrive. Within a week, their camp had grown to several hundred men, with more on the way. There were almost one hundred women who wanted to join the fight, also.

Alvar rode at the head of the "Eastward Ho" cattle drive. Ranger assisted by keeping the herd together on the East-West road. The citizens saw the herd coming and closed the city gates to protect themselves. When Alvar arrived at the gates, he rose up in his saddle, lifted the staff over his head, and uttered the sacred words, "Im ano gaw bee wal." A bolt of lightning flashed from the tip of his staff, cleaving the city gates in two. The cattle were driven into the city. A stampede followed as they barreled through the city's streets. Citizens began to stream out the eastern gate, hoping to escape the stampede. Instead, they found themselves encircled by an army. They could not go forward nor turn back. Glamdor waited until most of the citizens had been driven out of the city, then announced,

You have been infected by an evil pandemic. We have come to drive evil out of your lives. Those of you who wish to accept Beauty and Grace, come forward now!

Almost one hundred people came forward. They were greeted with Beauty and Grace by Raven, as well as many of the villagers who had joined her. Those who remained, several hundred, stood in defiance of Glamdor's declaration.

"You have chosen!" Glamdor shouted loudly enough for all to hear, "We are going to cleanse the city and drive out evil. Your choice has led to your death!"

Glamdor waved his arm over his head, pointing to the sky. Bow, the Rainbow Dragon, flew down above them, circling, then with a mighty roar, breathed fire upon the recalcitrant. Wails and cries rose up with the smoke and ashes. None were left alive.

Great sadness filled the hearts of those who had joined the Circle. One woman asked, "Why must there be pain and agony when we are only trying to bring Beauty and Grace here?"

No one answered. Not Alvar, nor Glamdor, nor Raven, nor anyone else in the Circle. There was a very long pause. Finally, Alvar spoke,

"That question can be answered AFTER evil has been driven from the Middle World."

Chapter 35

Battle of The Chosen

The Valley

After the city had been cleansed, the company took stock of what lay ahead of them. They were only twelve leagues west of the Eastern Kingdom's capital. A rider, on a swift horse, could get there in one day, an army would take three. Their mission was to drive evil out of the Middle World. The Capital City of the Eastern Kingdom was evil's last stronghold. The pandemic had infected most of the city's residents. In addition to these residents, thousands of infected had fled to the city, hoping to be protected from Beauty and Grace, which had driven evil from their towns and villages.

Capturing the capital and cleansing the city would be a monumental task. Hundreds would die, many of them fighting for Beauty and Grace.

"There has to be a better way," said Laura. "We cannot sacrifice the lives of those who have been saved from the plague."

"On the other hand," Jack suggested, "Beauty and Grace ARE worth dying for. We will all die sooner or later. To die in the pursuit of Beauty and Grace is to die a noble death."

"Both of you are right. Many will die. But we must find a way to minimize how many." Glamdor continued, "Ranger, you know the lay of the land, what lies east of the city?"

Ranger drew a map on the dirt, showing the walls of the city, and the road east of the city that led to the sea.

"How far is it between the city and the sea?" asked Glamdor.

"Less than a third of a league," he answered.

"What is the terrain like between the city and the sea?" Glamdor continued with his questioning.

"Mostly flat," he replied.

"Tell me," Glamdor was seeking more information, "what is the terrain like between here and the city?"

"Mostly flat, with a narrow valley running north and south, about a league west of the city. The East-West road curves north around it."

"Aha!" said Glamdor, excitedly, "I have a plan. Raven, Rae, and I will go into the city, as we did in the very first village we encountered. Rae can be our 'governess', like she was when we stayed at the Golden Arch Inn.' Looking at Winston, Glamdor continued, "Of course you will be part of our troupe,

Winston. We will need your wisdom, as well as your strong back."

"That is not much of a plan," said Alvar. "Is there more?"".

Glamdor smiled, then said,

You will see. In the meantime, bring the volunteers east. Make camp one league west of the valley, keeping everyone hidden as best you can. Have Laura, The Hammer, Talgor, Ian, Jack, and Rae join you. Ask Talgor to bring Bow as well. Raven and I will return in seven days. When we do, be prepared to encircle the valley.

Alvar did not like that Glamdor did not disclose all of his plan. However, by now, he had come to trust him and his planning ability.

"Ian," Glamdor asked, "will you see to the organization? Can you make an army out of our volunteers?"

Ian replied with a smile, "Of course, I shall create the army of Beauty and Grace."

Ian's Beauty and Grace *was* his talent for organization. He set to work developing an organizational plan. His plan was to combine men and women into groups of twenty-five, most of whom would be from the same village or town. Each group was to elect a captain. Next, he combined four of the groups into a block of one hundred. Each block would be assigned a commander, whom Ranger would choose. In all, there would be fourteen commanders. Next, Ian assigned each commander a specific mission. One was logistics, another was quarter master, and a third was to support Talgor and Bow in the fighting. Yet another commander was assigned to Laura and The Hammer. That left ten commanders who would report to Ranger and Alvar.

By the following morning, Ian was busy implementing his plan.

Glamdor, Rae, and Raven left early that morning for the city. On their way, Rae slipped the leather band from her neck that held the Raven Stone.

"Here," she said to Raven, handing her the stone, "you will need its power for the coming battle." Raven took the stone and nodded. "You are right. I will," she replied.

They arrived, along with a flood of infected immigrants, an hour before the sun set. Upon entering the eastern gate, they saw that the streets were full of infected people. It was disheartening to see so much suffering and misery. They followed the crowd, which seemed to be heading towards the center of the city. As they passed by people standing in doorways, they inquired about the location of a livery for the ponies and Winston. Mostly, they were met with angry stares. A few made rude comments, like "How should I know?" They finally came upon a livery stable. Upon entering, they were met by a stableboy, who appeared displeased, seeing he would have more work to do. Raven perceived his infection was not serious. She dismounted and walked to the boy.

"Could you please feed and groom our ponies and this old mule?" she asked.

Winston did not like being called an "old mule". He snorted and even stomped his left hind leg in disgust. The boy looked at Winston with fear in his eyes. "Does the mule bite or kick?" he asked. "Oh no," replied Raven, "he can be moody, as all mules are, but deep down he is good-hearted. Here," Raven continued, taking the boy's hand and stroking Winston's neck with it, "see, he is gentle once he knows you." A smile grew across the boy's face. Evil began to recede from him. It was the first time an animal had ever cured a human of the pandemic. Winston gave a gentle bray, knowing he had cured the boy.

"I will care for your animals," his demeanor now kind and gentle.

Glamdor asked, "Is there an Inn nearby?"

"There are several, but they are all full or closed due to the pandemic," the boy answered.

"If you wish," he continued, "you can sleep in the hayloft. It is safe and warm."

"Thank you," replied Raven, in a kind and gentle voice.

"Tell me," asked Glamdor, "why are there so many people coming into the city?"

"They fear the Dragon and the Sharur. They believe they will be safe here. I will bring you food if you like."

"That would be appreciated," Rae said.

The three did spend a warm night, but found it difficult to sleep comfortably. Sticks of straw kept poking them each time they rolled over. The following morning, each went to a different market and began implementing Glamdor's plan.

Glamdor went to the bakery market. At first, he just listened to the conversations. There were rumors about Bow and The Hammer. He heard one man say that The Hammer had slain ten thousand people (men AND women) with a single blow. Others said the Dragon had burned down entire villages and towns. What Glamdor found most amusing was the story of a ten-foot-tall boy, whose face was scarred by a giant bear, which he then had killed with a flaming sword.

After listening to the tales, Glamdor approached a group standing next to a bread stand. They were arguing over the price of bread. Glamdor told the baker, who had about a dozen loaves left, "I will take them all." The seller looked at Glamdor inquisitively, and asked,

"Why do you want so many loaves? That is a lot of bread."

Glamdor answered, "I heard that the Regent's soldiers are taking the immigrants out through the eastern gate. Rumor is that they are being sent to the island where the pandemic first began. But once they are a few leagues from land, the soldiers are throwing them overboard, drowning them."

"Doesn't matter to me," said the baker, "I am a citizen, not an immigrant."

"So am I," Glamdor lied, "but how are the soldiers to know who is an immigrant and who isn't. I am stocking up on food and going west to the valley just beyond the city. I hear it is safe there."

Those within earshot heard Glamdor and quickly began to spread the rumor. Raven went to the linen market and started the same rumor. Rae went to the fish market. In the Capital City, fishmongers were old, vile, foul-mouthed women. They were known for their use of profanity. Rae was shocked by their vulgarity. Nevertheless, she bought a huge basket of fish and spread the rumor. The women were not at all afraid, but were delighted to spread the rumor, as it would keep the immigrants, who had very little money, out of their market.

By the end of the day, a trickle of people had exited the western gate, heading for the valley. The next day, the trio went to other markets, spreading the same rumor. A slightly larger crowd left at the end of that day. For several more days they continued spreading the rumor. On the last day, Rae and Raven took their ponies to markets, and loaded them up with all they could carry. Glamdor did the same with Winston, who snorted his dislike with being burdened by a heavy load. The three met in the city's main square. There, they continued to spread the rumor, and declared they were leaving before it was too late. A large throng followed them out of the city and into the valley. At the end of the day, almost a thousand more had left, and were also in the valley.

Alvar had sent ravens to monitor activity in the city. They reported that Rae, Glamdor, and Raven had led an exodus out of the city. A raven also was sent to tell Glamdor the army was ready.

Glamdor, Rae, and Raven slipped out of the valley after most of the infected were asleep. They made their way to the army encampment, guided by Alvar's raven.

Glamdor instructed the company and commanders,

Tonight, have the army encircle the valley. Raven and I will return there. In the morning, I shall speak to the people. Those that heed my words will follow Raven out of the valley. Let them pass. When you see Glamring's flame, Bow and The Hammer are to strike first. Then, send the army to smite all who resist. Any that give up are to be spared. They can still be saved.

Rae took Raven aside. "Here," she said, handing the Raven Stone to her, "you will need this tomorrow more than I will." Raven smiled and took the stone. "Thank you," she said to Rae.

Glamdor and Raven returned to the valley. They found a family group huddled around a campfire. Raven could see fear in their eyes.

"Fear not," Raven's words were consoling, "stay close to me and I will keep you safe."

She held the Raven Stone up for the family to see. The children were the first to be drawn to its mesmerizing glow. Beauty and Grace entered into their hearts. Smiles grew on their tired and dirty faces. Their parents saw the Stone's effects. They too were mesmerized by its power. Stepping over to Raven, the mother reached out to touch the Stone. Its power cleansed her immediately. She was free from evil. Looking at her husband with renewed love in her heart, she guided his hand to the Stone. He too was cleansed. They took a moment to gaze into each other's eyes. It had been a long time since they had seen each other's Beauty. He took her hand and whispered, "I love you."

The other adult family members saw the Stone's effects. The evil virus lurking in their minds told them, "Run for your lives! The Stone will destroy you!"

As they turned, ready to run away, the husband yelled, "Stop! Don't run! It is alright. I am NOT dead!"

There was hesitation and confusion. The remaining adults thought to themselves, "Should I listen to my own mind, or the husband?" The hesitation was all Raven needed to save them. Before they could make up their minds, she lifted the Stone over her head and loudly commanded, "EVIL BE GONE!"

Evil fled out of the two aunts, four grandmothers and grandfathers. The entire family was saved. For the first time in many, many months, they slept peacefully. Rae stayed with them for the remainder of the night.

The following morning, Glamdor mounted Winston and rode to the top of a knoll in the center of the valley. He spoke words that would be remembered in song and sonnet,

SALVATION is here! You no longer need to be afraid. The Chosen Ones have come. Fear no longer. We bring you BEAUTY and GRACE! Evil will be banished from the Middle World. Your lives will be filled with joy and happiness.

Raven reached for the Raven Stone. Holding it over her head, its light radiated throughout the valley. She spoke words of salvation,

"Follow the light. Follow the Raven Stone. Follow your path to BEAUTY AND GRACE!"

Raven turned her pony and slowly rode north, holding the Raven Stone high above her head, its light a beacon of salvation. The family group followed closely behind her. Others followed, some in groups, others alone. Several hundred in all left the valley, following the light of the Raven Stone into their new life of Beauty and Grace.

Sadly, many hundreds more remained behind. Glamdor's words and the Raven Stone had only served to enrage the evil within them. Their fate was sealed when Glamdor drew Glamring from its sheath. As he did, a violent rush of wind came from the east side of the valley's rim. The Sharur of Garwalda drove forth, smiting all in its path. At the same time, a deafening roar from The Rainbow Dragon raged from the west side of the valley. The dragon belched flames of fire, scorching many to death. Next came the howl of the army, as men and women raced down into the valley from all sides. Wielding swords and axes, all who resisted were struck down. A few surrendered. They were saved. By the end of the battle, many hundreds were dead, but many more were saved. They were fed, comforted, and given the choice of returning to their homes or joining the army of Beauty and Grace.

Thus ended the first day of the battle.

Chapter 36

Battle of The Chosen

The City

The dead and dying lay on the valley floor. A few were clinging to life, but would not renounce evil, which sealed their fate. Only a very few saw Beauty and Grace. Most of them died with a smile on their face. Only a handful would survive. In time, the survivors would become "Apostles" of Beauty and Grace. They would become heroes for their bravery in the final battle for the Capital City. Those who survived the battle would travel throughout the Middle World, proclaiming the power of Beauty and Grace. They were living testaments to its power.

Ian was hard at work reorganizing the army. There were wounded to care for, units to reorganize, new volunteers to train, food and drink to procure, and, most importantly, plans to devise for the invasion of the Capital City. He performed the work of three men. As hard as he worked, he still found time to join the Circle to help develop the invasion plans. The Capital City was evil's last stronghold. There were outlying regions of evil, including the island just off the eastern shore, where the pandemic had started. But the battle for the Capital City would be the last one for the army of Beauty and Grace.

The Capital City would have to be taken. The question was, "how"? The Circle looked to Glamdor for a strategy. "Here are my thoughts," he said,

A frontal attack would result in many needless deaths. I suggest we use guile. Rumors can be effective. Previously, as you remember, we started rumors that the Regent's plan was to rid the City of foreigners. This time, rumors could be spread about the impending destruction of the City. Rumors that the Rainbow Dragon and Sharur of Garwalda would destroy every home and building in the City. Those who lived through the destruction would be slaughtered by the army of Beauty and Grace. Of course, this plan will have to be carefully orchestrated. We need a plan to convince the citizens that death and destruction are inevitable, without actually destroying the City, and keeping death to a minimum. We would proclaim Beauty and Grace will save them. However, by now, we know that very few will accept it. For the vast majority who have already chosen evil for themselves, we need a different plan. I suggest we add to the rumor that the Sea Gate on the east side of the City will be safe passage. Citizens can exit there, believing that they will avoid the wrath of the Rainbow Dragon and Sharur of Garwalda.

A lively discussion ensued after listening to Glamdor's plan. Raven suggested that, properly done, the rumors would diminish the citizens' will to fight. Especially if they saw a way to escape. The problem, Ian and others realized, was that they had already spread the rumor that the Regent had sent people through the Sea Gate to their deaths.

The Regent had become aware of this rumor, of his soldiers drowning foreigners. He actually embraced the rumor. It was a way to rid the City of unwanted people who needed to be fed, housed, and in general, cared for. However, this would also put a financial strain on the City's budget, which he felt was unnecessary. So, in order to demonstrate his support of the rumor, he had his fleet of boats brought to the docks at the eastern shore. He even went so far as to have his troops round up several dozen foreigners and march them to the ships. None were actually drowned, but it added to the validity of the rumor.

Glamdor was aware of the Regent's activities. He suggested that they add to the new rumor that citizens could flee through the Sea Gate, where the fleet would take them to safety. In addition, the army would surround the City on three sides, leaving the east unguarded. Bow and the Sharur of Garwalda would converge on the City, striking fear into the hearts of the infected.

Volunteers who had survived the battle of the valley, were sought out. Citizens of the City were asked if they were willing to go back there and spread the rumors. It was a dangerous mission. Death was a real possibility. Ranger asked Ian to assemble the survivors, which he did. Ranger explained the mission, and ended by saying,

"We all die, sooner or later. Beauty and Grace is the ONLY cause worth dying for."

Every survivor volunteered. They became the "Apostles of Beauty and Grace" .

It would take Ian two days to organize the army and surround three sides of the City, which would give Raven, Glamdor and the Apostles adequate time to spread the rumors. The next morning, they entered the City and began spreading the rumors. During the night of the second day, Ian stationed the army around the City.

As dawn broke on the third day, the citizens saw that the army had surrounded the City on three sides. Later that morning, Bow swooped down out of the north. Her deafening roar was heard for miles away. The Hammer sent the Sharur of Garwalda to topple the tallest spires. Fear, already fueled by the rumors, became panic.

Glamdor's plan was to have Bow and The Hammer begin the invasion. As they were spreading fear among the citizens, the army would attack. Many citizens fled through the Sea Gate, making their way to the fleet.

The fleet's admiral was unaware of the rumors and had no idea citizens would seek refuge there. Seeing a mob approaching, he ordered the ships to slip their moorings and anchor far enough offshore to keep them from boarding.

The citizens found themselves trapped. By late afternoon, thousands had fled from the City and were unable to return, OR board the ships.

Alvar, speaking magical words to his staff, sent a lightning bolt that smote the western gate in half. The army rushed in. He did the same at the north and south gates. Glamdor was waiting inside the western gate to guide the army through the City streets. Raven was stationed at the southern gate, and the Apostles met the army at the northern gate. All three branches fought their way to the palace, located in the center of the City, which was in chaos as the army poured in. Many citizens fell to their knees begging soldiers not to kill them. Other citizens, filled with rage and evil, charged the soldiers. Most were killed, as were several soldiers. By the end of the day, most of the City had been captured. Only the palace remained under the control of evil. Ranger led a company of fifty soldiers and three Apostles to storm the palace. The fighting was fierce. The palace guards were professional soldiers, and fiercely loyal to their master. Moreover, they were deeply infected with the pandemic. For them, death was the only path. Breaking through the palace gates, the company of soldiers were besieged with a flurry of arrows first, then a savage charge by the palace guards. Fierce fighting ensued. One of the palace guards hurled his spear at Ranger's back. An Apostle jumped between Ranger and the spear. It struck the Apostle in his chest, killing him. He gave his life to save Ranger's. The company fought their way into the throne room. There, they encountered the fiercest of the palace guards, who were the Regent's personal bodyguards. They threw themselves at Ranger without any regard for their own lives. Another of the Apostles jumped in front of Ranger and yelled,

"In the name of Beauty and Grace, STOP!"

His words inflamed the guards' rage. They lunged at the Apostle, stabbing, slashing, and hacking him to death. His death was not in vain. The personal guards' attention was on the Apostle, which gave Ranger and the company time to encircle them. Surrounded, with no hope of survival and certain death to follow, they formed into a V shape and charged Ranger. They were all struck down and killed before the first guard could get to him.

"Come out!" Ranger commanded.

"Bram, is that you, Bram?" the Regent meekly asked, fearing for his life. "Please, don't kill me," he begged. Ranger replied,

"Will you kneel before me and swear that I am the true heir of the House of Brigina and rightful King of the Eastern Kingdom, the Kingdom of Brigina?"

Evil filled the Regent's eyes. The pandemic had infected not only his mind, but also his soul. He would swear to anything in order to keep evil, as well as himself, alive.

"Yes, I swear", he lied.

Ranger saw that evil had consumed the Regent. He would never relinquish the pandemic's hold over him. Ranger drew his sword over his head, and with a powerful blow, severed the Regent's head from his body. Thus ended the rule of the Regent, and began the rule of Bram, King of Brigina.

King Bram's first action was to pardon every citizen who had welcomed Beauty and Grace into their lives. Soldiers, led by the remaining Apostles, Glamdor and Raven, brought news of the new King and salvation to every quarter of the City. Those who accepted King Bram's pardon were free to return to their homes. Those who refused, or lied, were taken to the western valley. Alvar, flanked by The Hammer and Bow, addressed the citizens who had fled through the Sea Gate. They, too, were offered King Bram's pardon. Most accepted. Those who did not were taken to the western valley.

The following day, Glamdor Raven, and Alvar traveled to the western valley. Once again, Glamdor rode up onto the knoll. Again, he spoke of Beauty and Grace. Some accepted and were saved. Those who refused met the same fate as their predecessors in the valley, who had refused.

By the end of that day, which would be known as "The Day of Salvation", the pandemic had been mostly eradicated from the Middle World. There were a few small villages which remained under the influence of evil. The Apostles would bring salvation to them eventually.

The last bastion of evil was not in the Middle World. It was on the island where it had all begun.

Chapter 37

Battle of The Chosen

The Island

The plague was first carried to the island of Khanelia (can eel ya), twenty leagues due east of the Eastern City, capital of the Eastern Kingdom. From there it found its way to the Eastern Kingdom, as ships sailed between Khanelia and the mainland daily.

Garballa, the island's ruler and Queen, fortunately survived the pandemic. Her husband, the King, and all her children died, as did a small portion of the population. Most of the survivors were infected with evil. Garballa was one of the very few who actually recovered. She tried her best to cure the islanders but was successful with only a few dozen.

Khanelia was a small island, with only one port. Its name means great one's (Khan) island (elia). The port was located at the base of a harbor protected on both sides by natural jetties of land. These kept the waters in the harbor calm, even in the worst storm. The port city, Khaniska (can is kah), was the capital of Khanelia. Garballa's palace was located on a hill overlooking the city. Khaniska, meaning great one (Khan) city (iska), was a multicultural mecca. Traders and seafarers came from far and wide to trade their goods, bringing with them their culture and customs. Some even brought their families, or married Khaniskans, and made the city their new home. Zapatnu (Za pot new) brought his wife and seven children to start a new life in Khaniska. His was one of the few families Garballa was able to save.

The pandemic brought much of the island's commerce to a halt. As was the seafaring custom, bright red plague flags were flown at the harbor's entrance, warning of the pandemic. Without trade, the City had to survive on what could be produced on the island's land, which was not very fertile.

The Circle, as well as Ian, Talgor, Laura, and The Hammer gathered in King Bram's (aka Ranger) throne room to plan the last phase of the battle. The fleet could take them and the army to Khanelia. The question was, how many soldiers would be needed? Once again, the discussion revolved around avoiding unnecessary deaths. This time, it was Raven who came up with a plan. She suggested a small group sail to Khanelia. Glamdor, Raven, Alvar, Rae, Jack, Talgor, The Hammer, and Laura would go. King Bram and Ian would stay behind to establish law and order. Bow could follow after they arrived. Raven's plan was to bring both fear and safety to the islanders. Fear would come in the form of the Rainbow Dragon and the Sharur of Garwalda. Safety would come in the form of motherly protection of Raven's, Laura's, and Rae's words. The plan would commence at the palace, where they would first solicit the support of Queen Garballa. Finally, Raven said,

> A single ship, sailing into the Khaniska harbor, would not arouse suspicion. Queen Garballa could apprise us of the extent of the pandemic. If the army is needed, we could have the fleet bring it over. Otherwise, it would be much better to cleanse the island with a minimum of force.

Ian set his part of the plan in motion. A royal order from King Bram was sent to the fleet to be prepared to ferry the army to Khaniska. Ian asked for one hundred volunteers, if needed, to sail to Khaniska. To his surprise, over one thousand, every soldier in the army of Beauty and Grace, volunteered.

When all was ready, the company (Glamdor, Raven, Rae, Jack, Alvar, Laura, The Hammer, and Talgor) set sail for Khaniska. King Bram (Ranger) and Ian would remain behind to help prepare the army, if needed, to establish Beauty and Grace in the Capital City. The seas were rough. Most everyone became seasick. Only Glamdor and Raven remained unaffected. Upon arrival, the company made their way to the palace. Passing through the city, they saw that the pandemic was present, but not as devastating as it had been in other cities. "Queen

Garballa," Raven thought to herself, "has been very effective in keeping the pandemic in check."

The palace guards escorted the company to the Queen's throne room. They were greeted cordially, but with cautious skepticism. Raven spoke,

> Your Highness, we have come from the Capital City of Brigina, formerly the Eastern Kingdom, where we have vanquished evil. We come in peace. We come to bring peace to Khaniska. We come to drive evil from your kingdom.

Garballa was overwhelmed with relief to *finally* have help. She had been fighting evil all by herself. "At last," she thought, "evil will be driven out once and for all."

Raven outlined her plan and asked the Queen where to start.

"Here, in Khanelia," she replied, with a renewed air of determination and optimism.

The company returned to the city and began speaking to its inhabitants, telling them they had come to drive out the pandemic. To be cured, they only needed to find their own Beauty and Grace. They also warned the citizens that great harm would come to those who refused to take their advice. For the remainder of that day and the following day, the message was disseminated to everyone.

On the third day, Bow flew in. The Hammer also arrived, and unleashed the Sharur of Garwalda.

Seeing a fire-breathing dragon and the Sharur circling the city caused many of the infected to tremble with fear. They raced to the city square, where they huddled together. Queen Garballa, along with Raven, Rae, and Laura were there to comfort and free them from evil.

The remaining people, who had refused Beauty and Grace, ran to the dock, hoping to find boats they could steal, that would sail them away from the danger. What they found instead was Glamdor, wielding Glamring.

"In the name of Beauty and Grace!" he shouted, "I command you renounce evil!"

At that moment, Bow released a torrent of flames just beyond the pier, causing the surface water to hiss and boil. Most of the mob fell to their knees, begging not to be burned alive. Those who chose to embrace their own Beauty and Grace, were allowed to return to the safety of the city square. The few dozen who remained rushed towards Glamdor, with hate and rage in their eyes. Glamring slashed and smote many. The Hammer released the Sharur, killing all who tried to escape Glamring's fury. In only a few short moments, evil was vanquished! Although there were a few small villages remaining infected, evil was no longer a force in Khanelia.

Jack and Rae remained on the island to help Queen Garballa rout out the last of the infected and cleanse the island. The rest of the company sailed back to the Middle World, knowing their mission was complete.

Chapter 38

Aftermath

Rae and Jack stayed on the island to help Queen Garballa cleanse the last few villages. It would take a week before the last infected Khanelian was cured (or killed). During that week, Jack and Rae discovered the island's enchantment. They also shared their attraction to each other. Ever since they first met, they had affectionate feelings for each other. However, under the circumstances, it was too risky to express them. At the time, they did not know what dangers lay ahead. Tender emotions could get in the way of making rational decisions. Now that the pandemic had been overcome, with only a few villages still infected, they felt it was safe to express their true feelings for each other. And so it was, that standing on the western shore, watching the sun slowly set into the sea, Jack bent down on one knee and asked Rae to be his wife.

"YES!" she shouted with joy. "I thought you would NEVER ask!"

They returned to the palace with smiles on their faces. Queen Garballa suspected right away that they were in love. She prepared an Engagement Banquet for them and invited all the residents of the island. It would be known throughout the island as the "Engagement Banquet of Beauty and Grace".

By the time Jack and Rae left the island of Khanelia, the pandemic had been eradicated. The others had left earlier. Talgor flew back with Bow. The others went by boat.

When Bow landed at the docks, east of the Capital City, she said to Talgor,

I have granted your wish. Evil has been driven out of the Middle World. You must release me, for I wish to return to my cave in the Ice Mountain and take a very long nap!

"Don't you want to stay for the celebration banquet?" Talgor asked her.

"I don't eat human *food*," she said with a sly smile. "I eat *humans*!"

"Well, in that case," Talgor said, not wanting to be Bow's next meal, "I release you."

Her giant wings flapped, causing a windstorm that almost blew Talgor off his feet. She rose high into the sky, and letting out a deafening roar, flew away. Talgor was sad to see her go. He had a special place in his heart for her. However, her comment about eating humans reminded him she was a *dragon*. And as everyone knows, dragons cannot be trusted, even if you know them as well as Talgor knew Bow.

While the company was still on Khanelia dealing with the pandemic, King Bram asked Ian to create an administrative structure which would manage the Kingdom of Brigina (formerly the Eastern Kingdom). Ian's organizational skills were exceptional. He created a royal council of ministers. Each minister would oversee a specific aspect of the kingdom. His next task was to define the duties of each council minister. Finally, he arranged for a feast to celebrate the end of the pandemic. After everyone had returned from Khanelia, the feast was held in the Capital City square. Every citizen was invited. The royal table was placed on a dais facing the square. At King Bram's insistence, Glamdor and Raven were seated in the place of honor at the center of the table. Next to Glamdor was Alvar, while King Bram sat next to Raven. Jack was to be seated next to Alvar, with Rae next to King Bram. At the last minute, not being able to be separated, Jack moved next to Rae. The Hammer and Laura sat next to Alvar. Ian and Talgor were on each end.

"My dear subjects," King Bram addressed the gathering,

we are here, today, to celebrate our freedom from evil. We are also here to honor those who have made this day possible. I am speaking, of course, of those who sit with me here, at the 'Table of Honor'. It is my great honor to introduce the Chosen Ones, Glamdor and Raven. You see a young man and woman. What you don't see is the power of the Unicorn within them. They have brought Beauty and Grace back into the Kingdom of Brigina, as well as all of the other kingdoms in the Middle World. Within them is the power of the Great Queen. Power given to them by the Unicorn. The only power that could overcome evil and drive the pandemic out of our kingdom. I have commissioned this statue to be erected, here in the center of this square, in their honor.

As the King waved his hand, the statue was unveiled. Glamdor was riding Winston, Glamring high above his head, flames leaping from its edges. Raven was on the Unicorn, holding the Raven Stone as a beacon of Beauty and Grace. There was a gasp of awe, then thunderous applause and cheers.

After the crowd settled down, the King spoke again,

Glamdor and Raven were not alone in their perilous quest. Alvar, Jack, Rae, and I aided The Chosen. We formed the "Circle" of Six, bound together in our crusade to rid the Middle World of evil. Our quest took us through the Great Rift Valley, facing dangerous fell beasts. There, we were saved by The Hammer. We crossed mountains and raging rivers in search of the Unicorn Valley. Together, we drove the pandemic away from our shores. I have commissioned a second monument.

Again, the King waved his hand, and the second statue was unveiled. It was in the form of a circle, higher than three men. The name of each member of the Circle was etched on the sides of the statue. Over the top was etched "Herein lies Beauty and Grace". On the bottom was etched, "Together We CAN defeat evil".

Children ran through the Circle statue, playing and giggling. Feeling their *own* Beauty and Grace.

"Laura and The Hammer from the Kingdom of Di-Wal-Nach are our special guests," King Bram announced. "The Hammer saved us in the Great Rift Valley. Then he and Laura joined Rae in driving evil from their kingdom. They joined us to cleanse our own country. We are forever indebted to you."

The Hammer rose and held up the Sharur of Garwalda. It rose out of his hand and circled the square, leaving a rainbow-colored trail. The people once again erupted into applause.

King Bram stood up and called for Talgor to come forward. "This man, Talgor," King Bram said reverently, "deserves a special honor. He tamed the Rainbow Dragon, whom we affectionately named 'Bow'. However, we all know it is never safe to get too close to a dragon. They eat people, you know," the King said in a cautious tone. "It is my honor to award Talgor the 'Star of Glory', for his bravery and valiant efforts to drive evil from our world."

The King placed a metal chain holding a large gold star around Talgor's neck.

Last, but certainly not least, was Ian, brother of Talgor. The King spoke many words of praise about him. Then, he asked Ian to come forward. Raising his royal sword, Bram said, "I knight you Sir Ian, First Knight of the Ruling Council."

With that, the feast commenced. Beauty and Grace filled the square. It was a celebration that would be canonized in verse honoring Beauty and Grace:

Beauty
    in us all
Grace
    in our beauty
Circle
    in sharing Grace
Salvation
    in fighting evil
Together
    in joyous celebration
Find
    Your Beauty
Let
    It Shine.

Chapter 39

Homeward Bound

Glamdor and Raven did not realize the physical and mental toll their quest had taken on them. It took two weeks of recovery before they could travel home. The Hammer and Laura had left a few days before. Ian was to stay and govern Brigina. Talgor would ride with Alvar, Glamdor, and Raven, as far as the Norseland-Di-Wal-Nach road. Jack and Rae would return to Khanelia, where Queen Garballa was going to marry them.

On the day of their departure, King Bram arranged a "departure" ceremony, in which each member was given a gift. Unknown to Jack and Rae, King Bram had arranged, along with Queen Garballa, to give them a villa on the island. Ian was also given a villa on the eastern shore, where he could temporarily escape his duties as First Knight of the Ruling Council. Talgor's kingdom was awarded "Special Trade Partner", in which their two countries could prosper and trade together. Alvar, Raven, and Glamdor were each given the "Medallion of Friendship"

The end of a great adventure often brings sadness. This was especially true for the company, who had lived through so many dangerous experiences together. Knowing they were going their separate ways brought tears, hugs, and sad feelings. Ian cried uncontrollably with the departure of his brother. They said their goodbyes to each other. More tears and hugs followed. Finally, the time to depart was at hand. King Bram provided beautiful horses for the company to ride. Glamdor, looking at Winston, said, "I will ride Winston."

"Why?" asked the King.

"You may recall what Naomi told Winston, when we departed Alvar's cave," answered Glamdor. "In case you forgot, she said that she would make Winston into a pot roast if he did not return me safely."

They all laughed.

Mounting their horses, waving goodbye, they rode west, heading home!

The ride west was much different than before. Villages and towns greeted them with honor. Feasts were held, awards and medals were given to the company. The city of Grumpelton held a two-day celebration in their honor. It was good to see that Beauty and Grace had replaced evil.

After leaving Grumpelton, they followed the East-West road until it veered south. Then, they left it and followed the trail leading to the Valley of the Unicorn. They were greeted with great enthusiasm as before. Villagers escorted them to the city and up to the temple. Monks lined the street with smiles, cheers, and applause. The following day they rested, waiting for the Unicorn to arrive. When the moon was high in the sky, Glamdor and Raven climbed the knoll. He was there, his mane and tail glowing in the moonlight. Both Glamdor and Raven took hold of the horn and returned the Great Queen's power to the Unicorn for safekeeping. There it would reside until needed again.

Early the next morning, the company left the valley, riding north. They followed the trail Jack had taken, up to the Norseland-Di-Wal-Nach road. Arriving at the road, Raven had to make a decision. Talgor, her father, was going to return to the Norseland capital. Glamdor and Alvar were going to Kambuka. Which would she choose?

"Raven," Alvar said, "you came to me when you were a child. You came to be trained. You are no longer a child, and you no longer need my training."

"I know," she replied with tears in her eyes, for whichever road she chose, it would mean leaving loved ones.

"I must go with my father, and take up my role as Princess, and one day Queen of Norseland. I will miss both of you deeply," tears now streaming down her face.

Glamdor was also filled with sadness at the loss of his dearest friend. He loved her as the sister he never had. She loved him as the brother she never had. They embraced one last time.

"You will meet again," Alvar reassured them. "Your kingdoms will form an alliance. You will attend each other's weddings and other important ceremonies. Who knows, you might even find time to vacation together."

Those words brought a tearful smile to their faces.

"Then," Raven said, "it is not *goodbye,* but *until we meet* again."

With that, Raven and Talgor turned north and rode off. Glamdor and Alvar watched until they were out of sight.

"The last leg of our journey," Glamdor said to no one in particular. Winston turned south and off they went.

Glamdor and Alvar traveled south until they came to the East-West road. There, they headed west. With evil gone from the Great Rift Valley, they passed through without incident. There were sounds of fell beasts. But they were far away. Winston was in no mood to linger, so they rode straight through the valley without stopping, except for water.

They followed the road for several more days. The towns and villages they passed through were no longer infected. Since it had been months since they had been there, very few of the townsfolk remembered them, and those that did were grateful, but did not make a fuss. Glamdor was thankful, for he had already had a lifetime of feasts and celebrations. Winston's pace quickened when they were only a few leagues from Kambuka. He went from a trot to a gallop when the frontier was in sight.

They were home!

James Black

Chapter 40

Homecoming

Frontier guards sent a raven to inform Calvin that his son and Alvar had returned. It was not long before G and A came swooping down to join their brother.

"Welcome home!" the two boys exclaimed, flying circles around Glamdor and Alvar. "Come, fly home with us!" they implored, as they headed home. Glamdor lifted himself up in the saddle as he always had done when he was about to take flight. But nothing happened! He tried again. Nothing. Glamdor could no longer fly! He looked at Alvar quizzically.

"Why can't I fly?" he asked, confused and a little sad.

"You are no longer a boy! You are a MAN!" replied Alvar.

"It is true," added Winston, knowingly.

G and A circled down to Glamdor, asking, "Why can't you fly with us?"

Winston said, "Because Glamdor is no longer a boy. He is a MAN!"

Not quite understanding yet, G and A landed and walked alongside their brother and Alvar.

They were met at the palace gate by a throng of well-wishers. Calvin greeted him with hugs, pats on his back, and a hearty "Welcome home, son!"

Glamdor's Ma took him in her arms, holding him close to her. She wept. Her son was home, in her arms, safe. She never wanted to let go of him. He too wept, feeling how much he had missed her and how much he loved her. Calvin wrapped his arms around both of them. In that moment, all three felt the bond of love between parents and child.

Naomi, not to be left out, barged her way through the crowd, took ahold of Glamdor and looked him straight in the eye.

"Made-a-man ah yer did they? See-n dat ur tall-her n'stronger. Did dat ol mulee take good care ah ya?" She looked at Winston suspiciously, "Guess the pot roast will have t'a wait!" She took Glamdor in her arms, holding him with love and thankfulness that he had returned.

Winston snorted, then brayed. Looking at Naomi, he said, "I brought him back, safe and sound. You have no right to even *mention* pot roast!"

There was yet another feast. Naomi made all of Glamdor's favorites, including lollipop soup. He was weary from traveling and wanted to feel the warmth and comfort of his own bed. He excused himself and went to his room early. He slept in late the next morning. It was almost noon when Naomi brought him breakfast.

"Yer be-a need'n food. Dat long journeee made ya thin," she said. "Yer be-a need'n to fatten up."

Later that afternoon, Glamdor was walking in the garden when his Ma and Da came to him. "When you are ready, we would like to hear about your journey," Calvin said. It took several afternoons for Glamdor to tell the entire story. When he finally finished, he looked at his parents and said,

I have learned many things since I left home. I have learned the value of friendship. I have learned that *true* friends are rare. Their friendship must always be honored. I have learned that through trials and tribulations, one becomes stronger. Being away from you, Ma and Da, I have come to appreciate how wonderful you are. You taught me. You love me. You prepared me to become a man. A MAN who will always be your loving son.

Tears filled their eyes. They lingered in the moment.

"It is our, and every parent's desire, for their children to be filled with Beauty and Grace. Your Beauty and Grace are what we have tried to help you find. Both your Ma and I are filled with joy, seeing the man of Beauty and Grace you have become," Calvin told his son.

Seeing the man their son had become, Ma and Da had quiet tears of joy and satisfaction. Knowing that they had fulfilled their deepest and most sacred desire of guiding their child into the light of Beauty and Grace brought more tears of joy. For several moments, neither Ma nor Da could speak. All they could do was hold Glamdor and weep.

Finally, Ma wiped away her tears and asked,

"Why must there be evil? Why can't we just live with Beauty and Grace?"

With a wise and knowing smile, Glamdor replied,

How would you know someone, or something, is beautiful, if you did not have evil to compare it to?

One's good deeds, and their Grace, shine in the presence of bad deeds.

Fighting evil **IS** Beauty and Grace.

Made in the USA
Columbia, SC
07 December 2021

50418508R00180